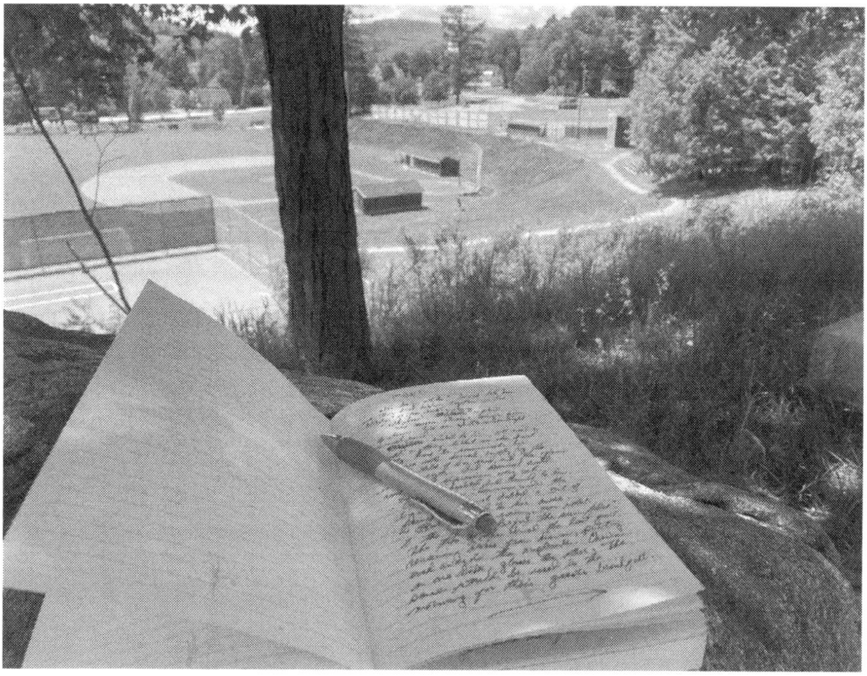

Jeffrey A. Richards

Hand In hand

First published by YouBeYou Publishing and Design Studios 2024

Copyright © 2024 by Jeffrey A. Richards

All rights reserved. No part of this publication may be reproduced, stored or transmitted in any form or by any means, electronic, mechanical, photocopying, recording, scanning, or otherwise without written permission from the publisher. It is illegal to copy this book, post it to a website, or distribute it by any other means without permission.

This novel is entirely a work of fiction. The names, characters and incidents portrayed in it are the work of the author's imagination. Any resemblance to actual persons, living or dead, events or localities is entirely coincidental.

Jeffrey A. Richards asserts the moral right to be identified as the author of this work.

Some historical context may appear accurate or inaccurate as is some names used by the author to depict characters. Any resemblance to actual persons, living or dead, events or some locations, is entirely coincidental and a product of the author's own imagination. The town of Littleton is mentioned as a historical location for the setting of the novel itself and meant to represent the town with fondness.

First edition

Advisor: Marilyn J. Merritt

This book was professionally typeset on Reedsy
Find out more at reedsy.com

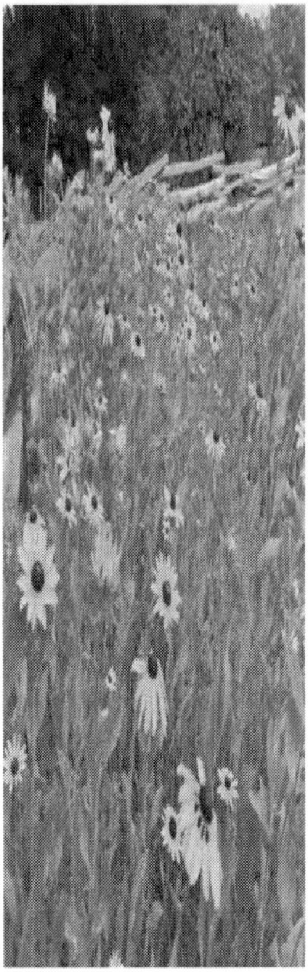

To those who have come before me, as far back as I can recall, and further back still. To those I call family, here today and yesterday as well.
To those I call friend from childhood, through the trials and tribulations of simply growing up. Lastly, for myself, for it had to be done.

To my daughter Calie Mae.
Grand daughters Marli Mae & Ava Grace.
Find your love & your passion wherever your path takes you.

For Marilyn. My girl.

Contents

I. HAND IN HAND 1
1. Introduction 2
2. Doctoring 3
3. Growin' Up 6
4. Fireflies 14
5. Where The Fabric Is Sewn 16
6. The Trip 18
7. Who You Are 22
8. The Sled 25
9. A Mother's Gift 29
10. New to Town 31
11. The Music Man 35
12. Mischevous 37
13. Being Young 40
14. First Kiss 43
15. Coming of Age 45
16. Finding Mary 47
17. The Ring 49
18. Hand In Hand 52
19. The Walk 56
20. A Fateful Decision 59
21. The Carousel 60
22. The Gazebo Affairs 62
23. Leaving 64
24. Overseas 66
25. Letters 75
26. A Night Out 78
27. A New Feeling 84
28. Mary's Fatigue 89
29. Faint Memory 90
30. A Father's Wish 92
31. Goodbye Samuel 95
32. Leaving Paris 97

33. A New Way 98
34. Learning to Write 101
35. Jogging the Memory 103
36. Waking 105
37. Finding Himself 107
38. The Decision 111
39. Revealing Himself 113
40. Wtih Child 115
41. Back To Paris 118
42. A New Home 123
43. Beautiful In The Morning 125
44. The Wedding 128
45. The Preparation 130
46. The Tired and Weary 133
47. Hello and Goodbye 137
48. Finding Home 142
49. Coming Home 146
50. Reuniting 155
51. Conclusion 158
Epilogue 160
Afterword 161

   1.
   2.
   3.
   4.
   5.
   6.
   7.
   8.
   9.
   10.
   11.
   12.
   13.

14.
15.
16.
17.
18.
19.
20.
21.
22.
23.
24.
25.
26.
27.
28.
29.
30.
31.
32.
33.
34.
35.
36.
37.
38.
39.
40.
41.
42.
43.
44.
45.

46.
47.
48.
49.
50.
51.

52.
53.

I
Hand In Hand

"I will take you…
…to the New England foliage where the leaves fill the rivers with the dropped colors of leaves of home;
….to a mountain of the highest of tops where the silence reverberates through the stillness of the night, where nothing is heard but the heartbeats of the other;
….to a place where I watch you gasp, and smile, and gasp again, and, for the first time in your life, gasp for more.

1

Introduction

Placing the pen in the folds of the notebook and closing it shut, I looked out across the open field from the enclosed porch. It was not lost on me my great grandfather had done the very same countless times. And his father, my grandfather, as well as my own father before me. I did not know them, but my father, I did. And I recall vividly our talks about this, that, but mostly about the land and where we came from. The vantage point from where I sit now has not changed for generations. The open field is still there, as is the place which I live. The hotel on the hill from which I learned everything has long been gone. From a father, a mother who left us all so young for the Heaven above, and the man to which I am named. With my boyhood days behind me, I am in the withering days of a life that has brought me plenty; happiness, despair, frustrations. And I recall it all. Specific days of being in school, swimming at the river, of Mary and I. Yes. Of Mary and I. Some of the best memories. The giddiness of young love, the anticipation of courtship and sipping ice cream sodas-two straws, one glass. The way we held hands. Pointer finger curled around the pinky. Small moments that might be well forgotten by some, but etched in my brain with fondness. The simple times are most always the best of times. And then there are the years overseas. Monique, my greatest love. Gone these past three years. Leaving behind hundreds of clay pottery she made with her own two hands, scattered in various places about the hotel. A lifetime of building together. It is here which I start. A journey of youth through the years of not knowing where to turn, to finally finding that destination of knowing who you are. A simple story during a simple time that slowly became more complicated and difficult. As I take a final sip of coffee from the mug which my wife made with her very own hands, it comforts me to pick up the pen once again, and put the story which I have been carrying around inside of me to paper.

2

Doctoring

The little town in the northern mountains of New Hampshire was home and a get away destination to thousands of people, who both lived and worked there, and found their way for other reasons. Those other reasons often led them folks back time and time again, eventually even calling the little town home. Most everyone who needed a job were able to find work, whether it was in the many small shops along main street, at the Saranac Glove Factory, where the world's best deer skin gloves were made and shipped around the world; at the coffin factory, where skilled carpenters were always needed; The Scythe Factory; the many tack and livery stables across Grafton County; or as brick masons and dam makers to maintain the six or seven different dams that supplied power up and down the Mighty Ammonoosuc River, from south Whitefield down into Lisbon itself. Folks worked, made money, paid their bills, raised families, came and went and visited and entertained themselves as often allowed. The town bustled and hustled, from its incorporation in seventeen eighty four, through the civil war years, the turn of the century, and what some folks thought to be a world war in Europe against Kaiser Wilhelm.

Things progressed greatly along that timeline, perhaps most notably the automobile. Horse and carriages were still a common everyday commodity, but the auto was seen much more regularly, particularly in the more heavily populated cities and towns across the North Country. At any given time William Dickson Brown, visiting from Pennsylvania with family and certain friends of notoriety in the corporate world, famed Edison and Ford to name but two, could be seen motoring all over while visiting his beautiful Highland Croft summer home. The horseless carriage along with the horse drawn carriages and wagons seemed to mesh together in society with hardly a care. However, every now and then there were still those minor accidents. Old Dr. Bugbee, his practice being on the corner of Maple Street, and just below the famed Maples Hotel, always had patients lining the porches. If he was not available, then his assistant Samuel Ishmael Sargent would take in the patient, addressing their ailments and concerns, setting up appointments with Dr. Bugbee if needed.

"Daddy, what's a meeting house meeting?" I asked one morning.

"It's a place son. Up on Meeting House Hill. It's where a small group of men meet to talk about how the town should or should not be run." Daddy explained.

I nodded a little at that, still not sure. Apparently Daddy recognized my confusion, like he almost always does, and explained further.

"Every two years, elections are held to vote in selectmen. Anyone male at least the age of twenty-one can declare their candidacy. The people in town vote who they think would be the best person. Just like voting for the president of the country. Sometimes the same selectmen win back their elections while sometimes new selectmen are elected. If you think back, I ran last year and was elected. So did Dr. Bugbee and Mr. Robins, the Chairman of the Town Committee." Daddy said further.

Daddy would explain things to me this way. Matter of fact in words he knew I might not understand. He would say if I didn't get use to hearing those words I would never understand them. He believed in formal education, but also believed that all education started at home with the parents.

"I remember. I colored some posters to hang around town for you. Mr. Harold down at the barbershop still has one hanging on his wall." I said.

Daddy chuckled at this. "Hmmm, does he now? Might be worth something someday or at least make a nice dart board." Daddy laughed harder.

"Nobody gonna toss darts in my Daddy's face." I exclaimed then added. "What will you talk about tonight?"

"Well, a man from the dam building crew will tell us how the progress is going on the rebuilding of a small section at the Apthorp dam. And Mr. Robins will give us the report on the fundraising for next years Fourth of July Celebration. And what this years Christmas parade will look like." he said. "I want to be in both parades again this year Daddy. Decorating and riding my bike with my friends is really fun." I said excitedly.

"I'll be sure to let Mr. Robins know that son." Daddy replied in response.

As we walked hand in hand through town, pass the Carnegie Library, passing the Ira Parker house, Thayers Hotel, Dr. Bugbees house, and up the short hillside to the Meeting House, the giant elm trees that lined main street began losing their leaves, perhaps a little early than they should. It became a game to find the largest leaf or the loudest crunch when we stepped on one. After sometime walking in silence I looked up to Daddy.

"Momma use to pull me on my sled here going to Grammy's house." I said expectantly.

Daddy looked down at me, his hand still grasping my own. Bending down on one knee, he looked me in the eye with meaningful eyes. "Don't ever forget that son. Ever. That's how you keep mommy alive."

I nodded.

Climbing the five short steps of the Meeting House, Daddy again told me the rules. That when we entered I was to stand in the back and not make a sound. When the meeting started

I was to come right back out and sit on the top step to wait for him. I was not to go anywhere else. And if someone addressed me, I would say 'Yes Sir' or 'Yes Ma'm' politely.

As I took off my fall jacket, placing it on the chair, I looked around. There was Dr. Bugbee and Mr. Robins and Mr. Harold too. Two others sat off to the sides, one holding a notebook and the other making coffee it looked like on the stove in the corner. Mr. Robins spoke first saying, "Alright, alright, lets come together. The quicker we start the quicker I get home to Alice's meatloaf she made tonight for supper. First order of business is last months business. Tom, read out the minutes from the last meeting will ya?"

Mr. Harold began reading. I made a note to remember that his name was Thomas, not that I would ever call him that. That wouldn't be polite.

"Yes Sir Mr. Robins" said Mr. Harold.

Just then, even before Mr. Harold could get out another word, Ishmae, Dr. Bugbee assistant, opened the door with a loud bang, closing it abruptly, rushing into the room.

"Beg pardon gentlemen. But I have urgent news. Really for Dr. Bugbee." said Ishmae.

Turning to the doctor to which he assisted Ishmae continued.

"Dr. Sir. There's been an accident." Ishmae stated quickly.

"Wonderful timing. What is it this time?" Dr. Bugbee asked exasperated.

"Ariel. That's Ariel Holmes, a good friend of mine, he works over at the lumber yard, it seems he was piling some newly cut board, the pile fell over on top of him. The foreman came by the office so I went over to look at the situation. He's bleeding from his head real bad. Real bad. I wrapped it and told those who worked there to keep pressure and keep him awake until I got back with you. Seems he got hit so hard it broke his false teeth and cut his mouth all up too." Ishmae explained.

"Ha. Perhaps he'll stop talking about his wife then and her spending habits. I listen to the gossip about town. His head injury probably isn't serious. One always bleed heavy from the head when cut. Nevertheless, I'll grab my bag." Dr. Bugbee replied.

"I already got it in the buggy Dr." Ishmae said.

"Gentlemen. This meeting is adjourned until tomorrow night. Same time. As you leave I suggest you keep old Ariel in your prayers." Dr. Bugbee stated as he gathered his coat, crossing the room, and leaving with Ishmae.

And just like that, my first Meeting House meeting was over.

3

Growin' Up

The bedroom window looked high above the small town, towards the flickering street lamps of main street and the surrounding neighborhoods, tree lined with rutty dirt roads, friends and family. A lone light shined through the third floor window, illuminating the bedroom which I called my own; a beacon from the other side of town, like a lighthouse lighting the course. My name is Samuel, and I'm fourteen years old. I live here, in a small northern New Hampshire town, high in the White Mountains, where nothing of interest happens yet folks come from all over to visit, and yet, still, the people who live here go about their daily lives in this quiet and serene community. I'm not like most teenage boys. Although I do like fishing with friends, and swimming at the river that flows through the middle of town, I enjoy being alone more, sitting in my room, high above the hotel guests, at the small wooden desk my father purchased for my twelfth birthday; writing stories, flipping page after page of Big Chief writing tablets; reading books, turning pages that I would imagine would hold my own words some day, in leather bound hardcovers, held by hands that I do not know. Stories about myself, the hotel which I live and where I sit to write about the place I call home; about my father, my mother, the townspeople. I have a clear view of the drive down below, the road that winds up to the wrap around porch, where summer gatherings occur, and traveling businessmen sit and read their papers. Folks from all over stayed with us. Coming up from Boston on the rail car, or coming down from Quebec City or Montreal. Whatever their length of stay, I would imagine their reasons for such travel, and imagine myself in a lone adventure. When I was younger I would ask my father where all these people came from and why they didn't have a home of their own. He would explain folks were meant to travel, sometimes in search of answers, sometimes to ask questions. I never knew what that meant of course. Not until this past birthday anyway. Now that I'm older, father giving me more responsibilities around the hotel, I compared our guests from afar to that of characters in books that I have read. Like Tom Sawyer or Captain Nemo, or Tom Thumb in the land of the Lilliputins. Imaginary places where real people invested themselves on personal quests for lost treasures and old ancestors. And I know that someday I will have my own personal quest and adventure. Whatever it may be, where ever it may be, I hope it's in a place with a hotel like this one. So I sit here and write my story. The early parts through the teenage years, with me and Monique and Mary and my son

Barnett Ishmael named after my father of English descent. My mother was Elizabeth, God rest her soul, being called home to the Lord she praised daily when I was only five. She was French Canadian and died of tuberculosis. I am an only child but have many cousins, aunts and uncles. My grandmothers live near but my grandfathers I never knew, having passed on before I was born. I know their names, know their faces, have heard their stories through many family members. Each year we visit their graves to lay flowers. My father would take me to visit these people frequently but the one I really enjoyed spending time with was Ishmae. My namesake. I was named after Old Ishmae. Samuel Ishmael Sargent is his full name, but folks here in town call him Ishmae and he likes that. Ishmae works at the hotel on the weekends, mowing the front lawns and trimming the hedges, repairing broken shutters or creaks in the steps and floorboards; to climbing to the roof placing slipping shingles back into place. He's been working for father for a long time, since before I was born. Ishmae is also Dr. Bugbee's personal assistant. He's been with Dr. Bugbee for near forty years or more. At almost seventy years of age, Ishmae doesn't look a day over fifty. Father says the day I was born, Ishmae was there and delivered me. Dr. Bugbee was down south in Concord that day and I decided to arrive in the world earlier than expected. It was Saturday afternoon and Ishmae was washing the second story windows. When he heard mother cry out, he rushed down the ladder and around back to the kitchen door knowing exactly where to find her. Mother was snapping beans for the guests' dinner. By the time he got there, a pile of green beans were spilled across the kitchen floor and mother was kneeling on the floor as well, the chair tipped over. Ishmae didn't hesitate to bring her to the front sitting room where he laid her on the sofa, politely asking one of the guests to have a seat elsewhere or perhaps the front porch would be more to their taste. Father came down the stairs and together, and between the two of them I came into the world. Mother immediately called me Samuel as she held me against her chest. Father says that made Ishmae smile from ear to ear. That was the year eighteen hundred ninety-eight, in the summer, five days before the Fourth of July.

 A small framed man for his size under six foot, he was well known around town for his faithfulness as Dr. Bugbees assistant and as a towns person. Never missing an opportunity to help the ladies with gardening or moving porch furniture and never missing Sunday services at the Methodist Church on main street, Ishmae became even more popular the next day after I was born. The praise mother and father placed on him ensured him a favorite place at the hotel for as long as he wished to stay on. And so he did. On the third floor, in the room which I write now. From before I could walk Ishmae and I were connected, both in name and popularity. At night, instead of reading me stories, he would tell me of his own childhood living in South Carolina with his mother and younger brother. And on Saturday afternoon he would take me with him to the market to pick up vegetables for the week. And when we weren't busy, he'd take me to the river to whittle sticks to a sharp point and teach me bow to spear fish. Next to father and mother, Ishmae was my teacher from the very beginning. He would tell me stories of his own boyhood days down south. What it was like to live on a plantation. To be an indentured servant as he called it, myself not really understanding what that meant. He said it was like being tied to a chain like a dog in a yard; only so far you could go before it was yanked hard. That chain broke the day he left the land he was born on with Dr. Bugbee and traveled north. On that day he discovered a new way of life.

He was born in 1850, South Carolina, Charleston County, next to the Ashley River. The land produced the "southern gold" rice, Samuel Ishmael Sargent worked the paddies from the time he could walk a straight line until the war ended in '65. He was fifteen years old then, a young man on a plantation of nearly three hundred enslaved. He lived with his mamma the entire time, she being a house servant, therefore their cabin was a two room with a real potbelly stove and outhouse in the back. The luxury of being on staff morning and night to the Big House. His mamma and he shared the back room right up til he was eight, then she moved to the front room so he could have the room to himself. He missed her for the first few months. Missed lying in bed with her as she told him stories of her village across the waters; her mamma and pappa and brothers, her grandparents who she adored, especially her grand mamma who taught her how to ground meal and make water gourds. They would also stare up at the deep night sky and count the shiny dots. Stars she called them. She became his lone teacher, and being able to read a little bit herself, she taught him as well. The bible was the only book he would ever hold until much later in life and the bible became his verse and song from front to back. He loved reading the passages. Though he stumbled and didn't know a lot of the bigger words, the words his mamma did teach him he knew well so could pick up the meaning of most things written. They would take turns reading. He loved all those stories then and missed the voice to which they were told immensely. His father he never knew, not from the time he was born, or ever. He only knew he held his first name. A testament of no ill will from mamma was held against him for his disappearance. It was the end of a very long war, to which life became ever more hard for him and the other slaves in his little cabin community along the river banks. Stories circulated nightly around small fires that spoke of emancipation. He didn't understand what it all meant, other than he and his mamma would be able to leave the plantation if they so wanted. Some spoke of leaving, of heading north, of following a drinking gourd. He knew about gourds from his mamma's stories and was confused how a person could possibly follow one. It wasn't until a short time later, in the spring of 1866, when he realized the drinking gourd was made up of stars in the night sky by tracing and connecting one to the other, and if you kept your eye on the brightest star in the sky, which made up the handle of the gourd, it would lead you north and north was freedom. In the north you could do whatever you wanted. You could even buy with money from a job which paid you a four room cabin. The more he thought of that idea the more he became excited. Mamma told him to push those thoughts away. They had everything they needed right here on Magnolia Plantation. She had a job and the Master and Mistress treated her well. She particularly enjoyed the Mistress' company and hers. Though it was unusual for both servants and the Mistress of the House to have any kind of cordial relationship, they did. Perhaps it went back to when mamma first came to Magnolia from across the river, with infant in hand. The two plantations came to agreement that mamma would now live there, separate from the other slaves, in a cabin of her own to raise the child and that she would never see her own mamma and pappa and little brother again. Mamma never spoke of it and Samuel never asked. She was only twelve then, very young. Perhaps the Mistress saw her own daughter in mamma. The daughter she lost when she was only twelve to smallpox. Perhaps that is why mamma' stance on leaving was not to. She was simply grateful and held an affection towards the one who taught her how to read, write a little, and assured her safety and well being as a servant at the Big House. Samuel, as the infant would be named by mamma, would also have a middle name, Ishmael, chosen by Mistress herself. Again, unusual, considering the circumstances.

"Yes Sir Dr. Bugbee. Your supplies are in the carriage. I also took the liberty to pack a couple extra liverwurst sandwiches for the trip.", said Samuel.

"Samuel. You are going to make me fat.", replied the doctor.

Samuel looked to his employer, a slight smirk, his eyes moving from the Dr.s' eyes to his midsection, a girth that could already stand to lose twenty pounds.

"Yes. Dr. Bugbee. You are right.", said Samuel.

Dr. Bugbee smirked back, turning and huffing slightly. Once atop the carriage, reins in hands, "Now I'll be back in a couple of days. I'll be staying with the minister up in Bethlehem if you need to reach me. He doesn't have a telephone so I suppose if it's important enough you'll need to come yourself. I've left instructions on how to tend Katherine Davis. The baby isn't due for a few weeks yet. If she continues to have labor pains, have her continue to take a teaspoon of tincture once a day. There's an extra bottle in the cabinet. You know where the key is."

"Do not worry Dr. Bugbee. I know what to do.", replied Samuel.

"I know you do. I've taught you everything I know.", the doctor replied back.

Sitting up a bit straighter, Dr. Bugbee, the only doctor in a fifty mile radius, and the only doctor who comes close to qualifying as a surgeon if needed, yanked the reins, giving a tug and small slap to the lone, pulling horse.

"Hee Haw. On Jakob. Giddy up."

Samuel watched his employer and friend cart his way down the hard packed dirt and rutted main street, heading northwest towards Bethlehem.

Back inside the Victorian home of Dr. Bugbee, located on Main Street, across from the Masonic Temple, Samuel tidied up the breakfast cutlery. He then double checked the key to the medicinal cabinet, noting it was in the familiar place as it should be. Today was Thursday morning, and like all Thursday mornings Samuel attended the farmer's market at the other end of town in the little village of Apthorp. He always walked, with a wicker basket cradled in arm, as he enjoyed meeting friends and neighbors along the way. Only a few steps down the street he would most always meet with Elizabeth Heald who worked the morning shift front desk at the Thayer's Hotel across the street.

"Morning Ms. Heald. Such a lovely summer morning.", Samuel said.

"Now Samuel. We see each other most every morning and each time you say the same thing. Why don't you ever say anything about my new hat or how lovely the flowers are that I pick from my own garden beds for the front desk?", Ms. Heald replies in a teasing fashion.

"Ms. Heald, beg pardon. But my mamma raised me right. If I did such a thing gossip would certainly take hold and before you know'd it the whole town be talkin' about how you and I were carrying on talking sweet on each other.", Samuel said back.

Ms. Heald looked at him, with a look of almost embarrassment and surely would be so if she hadn't followed the look up with her reply back.

"Samuel, you don't need to use any more sugar in your sweet treats than you do in the words you choose.', she said with a smile and a gentle touch to his arm.

"Just trying to keep the town from talkin' Ms. Heald.", Samuel replied with a laugh. "But if I were to give you a compliment I would say somethin' like 'Ms. Heald, the hat you wear and the posies you carry are nothing but beautiful but do not compare at all to the way you carry them."

And with that, Samuel would continue his way, leaving Ms. Heald with a cup full of happiness and a smile that would last the full day.

And so it went, down the tiny main street in his sojourn until he would pass by the Town Hall, looking up to the clock to gauge his progress. If the time were past 9:35 he would know he would be arriving at the Apthorp Common at 10:05. To make the farmer's market on time and be assured to get the freshest and ripest of vegetables he most always set his mind for a 9:50 arrival. Some morning folks talked a little more than usual.

Samuel has always enjoyed the early morning. It's quiet then. Before folks began milling about going here and there, to and fro, about daily business. It reminded him of his youth, when he left Magnolia Plantation, leaving his mamma behind despite begging her to go with him. Of course, he already knew her answer each time he begged. She understood his need to leave. So the two parted ways in the spring of eighteen sixty nine, heading north, up the coastline, where he was hoping to make better travel time and kinder folks along the coastal fishing villages. The war between the states had ravaged the entire country, the country he had never seen. He had never traveled further than across the river to the plantation where he was born. He went there once, with a group of two other slaves, by wagon, delivering barrels of corn. He unloaded and that was all. Saw just enough of the place to want to turn and go back home. That was when he was eighteen. The thought of ever living anywhere else, despite his wishes, was not realized. In only four short years, at nineteen years of age, he would find himself aboard a whaler heading up the coast to Boston.

And here he found himself. In a place he never knew existed and would never think of imagining. In a town alongside a river, up north in a state he knew nothing of. Working for old Dr. Bugbee, who he owed his entire life of gratitude, if not his very life, was rewarding and educational. He learned something everyday. From fixing just the right amount of tincture to remedy arthritis to setting a splint on a young one who fell out of a tree. If not for Dr. Bugbee, and had he not been in Boston that day, there was no telling what would have happened to him. Working the whaler from Charleston the fall before, sailing up the waters called the Atlantic, as he learned, hunting the great Right Whales, of which there were vast amounts, like cattle in a pasture, he stepped off the whaling ship with no idea what to expect in America's founding city, but with the most money he ever had clanging in his pocket from killing those whales, he felt the richest person in the world.

Dr. Bugbee was a gentleman. Not a southern gentleman, whose air of sophistication shined through his demeanor and posture, head tilted forward and peering over glasses while one hand rested on the lapel of his jacket, the other on the cane he didn't really need but carried with him to top off the appearance of arrogance and wealth and dominion, but a northern sophisticant who graced the ladies with flowery speech and gives nickles to the little ones for licorice and sarsaparillas.

Samuel Ishmael Sargent, or Ishmae as he was called, was the only colored man in the entire state, or so it certainly felt to him. Surely, in all the northern parts which he visited with the doctor while he made his doctoring rounds from town to town, house to house. But he was accepted. An entirely new experience and feeling compared to where he was born, raised, worked, and witnessed many travesties and afflictions against people the same color as he.

At barely the age of twenty, Ishmae stood just under six foot, with a slender and slight frame that gave him long strides and a giddyup in his hitch as his momma use to say to him. With dark, curly hair and a smooth face he appeared every part of being even younger.

Because of this the even younger boys around town took to him right away as part of their club. Ishmae fit right in, showing them all how to whittle down a stick to stab fish or what tracks bobcats make, or lending a hand whitewashing fences and buildings.

And so it was for Samuel Ishmael Sargent. Almost a foreigner in a foreign part of the country. When he first came to our hotel on the hill Momma and he made quick friends. He was always willing to lend not only his hands in fixing and mending but would stop by just because he was 'in the area' as he would tell her. And she would gratefully and delighted fully serve him up pieces of apple and blueberry pie in thanks and kindness of his time and gestures. Daddy appreciated him as well, for he added a certain culture around the place as he put it. Not because of the color of his skin but for his southern upbringing and a time when things were not perfect. Daddy said Ishmae was the model for which we all should be striving towards. Hardworking, dependable, reliable, trustworthy, and a sense of serving the common good for all. My friends and I could see that, but mostly we liked having him around for his stories and sometimes taking us on adventures around town. Like most kids we all liked walking the rail lines, balancing our feet on the rails, contesting each other how far and how long we could keep a balanced straight line. Like most things, Ishmae had a story about that too.

The iron rusted tracks stretched across the county line like the black top pavement that weaves in and out of the hollows and valleys, over hills and grassy green dales, both transporting its passengers to places near and far. One, weathered with red rusty flakes, the other pot marked and oily stained, signs of overuse by those moving along in their lives.

We, as kids, tightened up the laces of our shoes as we placed each, one at a time, on the ancient rail. For we knew this course well. This path we all took many a journey down. We made ready for the pilgrimage, always made every weekend afternoon. A childhood playground where you can only look back to where you came from and look ahead to where you want to go.

Placing each foot carefully on the slim rail, we found our balance, taking the first steps of many. It was always the first step that held our concentration the most. Never the second, or third, or fourth or fifth. Always the first. For that first step to anywhere caused one to swallow hard, squint a little harder, breathe a little deeper just before lifting heel to toe; holding that first breath, until its release and then the second, realizing we were on our way.

As the iron rails grew accustomed under the soles of our feet, our thoughts drifted to other notions. Autopilot takes over, with a dashing of ideas, a smattering of concerns, life's problems left unsolved. Each step on the rail was equally as important as the next, as we became so entranced with the simple act of walking, our minds became caught in a meditative moment of pure tranquility. Sights, sounds, smells around us blurred into the crevices of our mind, lost in a sojourn of wanderlust and happiness. For like the travelers before us, the unbalanced forces of life's greatest demons can only be defeated by the sheer will of a balanced and concentrated effort to persevere and survive. With each step was another victory and reason to celebrate.

The rail bed below us, lurks thigh high with weeds. The weeds that reach up with their flora and fauna blades, attempting to distract, but failing always. For to slip, to waver, to become distracted by the smallest of challenges, will often lead to our stumble, the downward fall that is difficult to stop, falling into the pretend quicksand of our childhood days. Starting over again, when we had come so far, we knew it would be difficult. However, our eyes had never left the spiritual guide that moved us forward. So we did not fall. We walked the straight line as far as we could. And when we did stumble, or lose balance, we quickly hopped back to try again, our concentration even deeper then before.

Ishmae taught us these things. He taught us to persevere and not give up. To keep going. And if the time of year was right, we'd bring along a bucket or two to pick the blackberries off the sides of the tracks. He said every endeavor needed to be rewarded.

4

Fireflies

Summer in the White Mountains surges quick and eventful after the April frosts and spring rains. The months of late May through the end of August are ones filled with swimming holes, rivers, so many lakes, fishing and canoeing, berry picking, wildflower pressing, and sojourning up the Presidential Range mountain peaks to look out above and beyond. Our hotel that sat on the hillside above town became the epicenter of everything summertime represented. Travelers from the bigger cities south and Canada came to us in search for just a little reprieve during these days. They'd stay with us for two, three, five, or sometimes even two weeks at a stretch. And they'd return each summer after that, sometimes even during the winter for the ski season. We got to know them well, personally, as well as a distant relatives that make their way for short visits together.

I had friends of course. In a small town where everyone knows everyone that can't be helped. Some friends better than others; our little club or gang as Daddy would call us. But it was always nice to meet with other kids from far away. During the summer at the hotel, I would look forward to seeing families with kids walk through the double front doors, sign the register at the front desk, and watch Ishmael carry their luggage up the stairs to the second and third floors. I'd look forward to seeing them mingle about on the front porch, playing on the hillside, churning ice cream for social events. But perhaps the best time was in the early evening, just as the last of the days light faded from the sky and the fireflies would dart about, their tiny lights blinking in flight. The kids and I would run about on the grassy hillside, or down in the park below, mason jars in hand, contesting one another on how many we could catch and bright our jars could become. Ishmae would often join us telling us kids stories of his own childhood days down south. He would never use a mason jar to catch the fireflies in, cupping his hands instead, moving slow so as not to scare them, watching as they wiggled and crawled about his hand. And when ready, he'd lift his hand, as they again took flight into the freedom of the evening air. He told us to always let them go when we were done catching. To keep such beautiful creatures would ensure their eventual death trapped in a glass jar and what purpose would that serve. And so we did. When hollers from the hotel porch would come for us to come in, it was always with empty jars. Sometimes our parents would ask where the fireflies were. Our answers were directed with a finger point "Out there" we'd say. The lesson was learned each summer. Repetitive.

Always the same, with the months in-between remembered and connected with a similar event. That was Ishame's way. Always a teacher. His lessons were not academic in nature, but in locked and firmed in nature itself. He would tell us that in nature we could find all the answers we needed to become successful and responsible. We just needed to look hard enough. He taught us without us even knowing it.

5

Where The Fabric Is Sewn

Her room was on the second floor, away from the guests but close to her family. It was her room and her room only as evidenced by the small, hand painted sign that read "mom's sewing room" cursively written with her own flourishing brush stroke in colors that resembled her bright and contagious personality. That's not to say others were not allowed in the room, on the contrary, her Thursday night ladies knitting club met without fail, except for one winter day in January, the year before the knitting stopped, when the snow became too much to trudge through. As the matron of the family home she took great pride in organization and keeping on time in a timely manner. This was particularly noticeable when it came to the hotel itself, from morning, noon, and night. From check-in to check-out she made sure her face and smile were the first and last a guest saw in their stay. She was in continuous motion, always busy, at this, or that, yet made it all look seamless and flawless. Nothing ever bothered her. Quite simply, she had a solution for everything if we trusted her. And trusted we did like a guiding faith standing on foundations of principles given to her as a child, which is why her room was her room only, a reward for dedication and steadfastness.

Four large floor to ceiling windows engulfed the room with constant and magical light for her hands to work the loom which she weaved, or the knitting needles which made the click-clacks that could be heard from the fifteenth stair before reaching the second floor. The sound became synchronous with the three-forty train out of White River Junction. A signal that meant things were as they should be and right on time. Doilles and afghan blankets, quilts and small, woven rugs skirted the hallways, sat under table lamps, and folded across the foot of beds for additional warmth and comfort.

When the room became quiet and the curtains drawn to shut out the sun rise over Mt. Eustis and the Presidential Range beyond; when the sign on the door hung a little crooked, no longer perfect; and when there was nothing but silence from the fifteenth step on, that's when the second floor became withdrawn, subdued, and vacant of the former brightness. Her death left a massive hole in their lives Samuel's father was no exception. Their love was reciprocated through adoration without shame nor fault and without question. Without her, meager tasks became high priority items of importance that would otherwise be mundane and almost meaningless. Still a husband, still a father, he kept her alive not only in heart but in joyous song and story. The large hotel and home never ceased in its musical declarations on summer afternoons or holiday parties. "Miss Susan Parties" became the anticipated date on everyone's calendars, as the hotel on the hill announced the latest of its affairs. Her love for music lived on with each turn of the Vitrola's handle, a task that brought great pleasure to Samuel's father. At night, when the stillness of the day faded, and the heat still clung to soft, billowing curtains in half opened windows, he told bedtime stories about her, her wonderful qualities, and undying love for them both.

And so Samuel grew to know her well. With a little boys love and a curiosity that often found him lost in her room, imagining her next to him, dark and dank, as it was. But just being in her space, where she regarded as sanctuary, surrounded by things he knew were hers, that she used, gave him a comfort, strengthening the bond between mother and son. He would sit at the loom, on the stool too high, his feet dangling, running his hands over the strands that she last strung. One day his father opened the a-jar door feeling, or imagining, a wisp of ethereal air escaping. With a trembling hand and a hesitant step, he entered, for the first time in more than two years. It was as it was. Nothing moved; nothing changed. But her presence and the sound of her. His smile of just being there hid and disguised the wet eyes for which he attempted to blink dry.

"Daddy?" said Samuel.

Startled, he turned toward the voice, to find his son of six behind the loom.

"Samuel. You…what are you doing in here?" Daddy asked.

"Telling stories Daddy. Like you. " replied Samuel in a little boy voice.

Wiping his cheek with the back of his hand Daddy said. "I see. Well then…that's good. That's good."

"I like it here." Samuel said.

"Me as well son. Me as well." Daddy said as he looked about the room. "Perhaps its time. " Daddy turned then, went to momma's curtains, pulling them back just the tiniest bit, allowing the first sliver of light to filter into momma's room for the first time in two years or more.

"She wants this." Samuel said then.

"You are right son. She does." Daddy replied.

"She wants it all back inside." Samuel said as his hands moved across the wool strands of the loom.

"We will do it for her then. And you can tell her more stories. In the light."

Father and son held hands then, surrounded by the fabrics she wove and sewn.

6

The Trip

"That's alright Ishmae. I completely understand. Your work with Dr. Bugbee comes first. You go and take care of that family up there in Lyman." said Mr. Anderson.

"Thanks for understanding Sir." replied Ishame in return.

The sun had risen over Mt. Eustis and the morning was in full affect as the birds were singing their daily songs. Samuel sat in the wicker chair on the front porch spinning the propeller of a toy model airplane he had built yesterday. His ears always perked up a bit more whenever Ishmae and his Daddy were talking. It just seemed as though the two of them had the most interesting things to say to each other. Like the time when they talked about how to best clean the clock face atop the town building. Daddy said scaffolding from the ground up would be the safest way but Ishame was confident using a harness down over the top would be better and less time. Or when the best time for fishing Perch Pond was. Morning or evening. Ishmae said it didn't matter, fish were fish and they fed the same at both times of the day. Daddy thought morning but Sam thought that was because he hadn't had breakfast yet. This time though it was about Ishmae not helping at the hotel today, instead being called away up to Lyman where there was a sick family. Any trip up that way, especially if it was all the way up on the mountain, would be an all day trip. And that's exactly why it sounded so inviting to Samuel.

"Daddy. Could I go? I mean, if it was alright with Ishmae?" Samuel quickly asked.

"Well, I suppose it is. If Ishame doesn't mind." Daddy replied.

"Oh no Sir. You know I do enjoy my time with young Master Samuel here." Ishmae said.

"Yippee! I'll go get my things." Samuel bellowed in excitement.

Samuel and Mr. Anderson turned to look at one another saying the same thing. "Things?"

It didn't take long for Samuel to re-join the two men in his life. With a small knapsack slung over his shoulder he was ready.

"I'm ready to hit the road Ishame. Are we taking the carriage or the Ford?" asked Samuel.

"Dr. Bugbee left the Model T. We can take that. Now before you ask, the answer is yes. You can ride behind the seat." Ishmae said with a laugh.

Without even a reply Samuel darted back inside, letting the screen door slam behind him. "Hold that door." yelled his father behind him.

"I best be leaving Mr. Anderson. It's a long ride." said Ishmae.

"That's a fact. Mind the river. The rain we had a couple nights ago raised up over the meadows from what I hear. I'm sure its receded but the roadway will be slick with muck." said Mr. Anderson.

"I will. Perhaps I'll bring a shovel for Samuel to clear a path. Will keep him busy." Ishmae said laughing with Samuel's father following.

Samuel returned, this time holding the door behind him. "Ready now?" asked Ishame.

"Ready." replied Samuel.

As the two namesakes descended the front steps of the hotel, it was not lost on Mr. Anderson that both of them, old man and young man, two Samuel's linked together because of the same woman, were also destined, it seemed, to be an integral part of each others lives. One old, nearing seventy something, and the other a newly turned fourteen, had become more than friends but companions of the same caliber. Young Samuel seemed to have an old soul quality in him that resonated with Old Samuel who relished telling stories of his youth and the places he had seen before coming to the White Mountains. And his son took to this storytelling, always carrying around a writing tablet and sharpened pencil. Being his father he understood the importance of having a mentor besides himself. As his son grew, becoming his own man, their relationship would surely strain and some head butting would surely happen as his son formed his own opinions. Having someone else who he could trust and confide in would help his son see different perspectives and perhaps understand the lessons he was learning more clearly. He himself had a mentor when he was Samuel's age. His grandfather was one of the most important people in his young life. Always willing to spend whatever time he had with him. And now, thanks to his wife, rest her soul, for seeing those same qualities in Ishmael. He was as important to him as he was important to his son.

They set out as soon as they made their way through town back to Dr. Bugbee's residence on Main Street. Gathering the necessary medical bag and a coil of sturdy rope, he handed them to Samuel to place in the Model T.

"What's the rope for?" asked Samuel.

"Just in case we become stuck in the mud. Your daddy was right. The road down at the Salmon Hole bridge gets muddy and mucky when the river rises." said Ishmael. "You crank it up and I'll start her up."

The first few miles were uneventful. The roads were clear, passing only a handful of other vehicles, some gasoline driven, but the majority horse and buggy. As they got further from the outskirts of town however and because it was still early in the day they did encounter a cow crossing from the farm on the town line crossing over to the pasture near the river. Samuel moved from the back of the truck to the front seat where he could count each of the cows. Sixty-seven black and white heifers.

"I worked a dairy farm when I was younger." said Ishmael. "Down near the Vermont state line. Little farm that sat up on the ridge. In Bradford. Hard work it is. 4:30 in the morning comes early." Ishmae stated.

"What was your favorite job Ishmae?" asked Samuel.

He didn't hesitate for a moment. "Whaling. Toughest job I ever had. Not for an old man like me that's for sure. You go out to sea. Sail all day and all night. Always something to do on board a ship. I was a rigger. That's someone who climbs the mast heads, securing the roping for the masts."

Samuel sat listening intently as he always done with one of Ishmae's stories. "Now listen. It wasn't the killing of the whales that I liked so much. But the quiet of the sea. When you're out there, just you, and as far as you can sea, just water all around you, it gives a feeling of how small and alone you can be. That's why the sea isn't meant for most folks. Folks are meant to be together."

"But you had others on board with you. Mates right?" asked Samuel.

"I did. And good…mates…where did you hear that word?" Ishame shifted to ask.

"I read Treasure Island in school. It was full of pirates and sea words." Samuel replied.

"Never heard of it. But yes. I had mates. Some good and some …well, not so good. But it was the sea Samuel. It was the sea that kept me close and safe all those days. We became good friends. At night, with the moons glowing path setting just atop the waters, it was as though it was leading me to somewhere. Like this road we are driving on now. It pulled me." he explained with a solemn inflection in his voice. Lost in the moment for a moment, he continued. "But no. No sir young master Samuel. It wasn't the taking of life from that whale that I enjoyed. He was just a dumb animal. It's all a slaughter really." Ishmae ended.

"A path." was all Samuel said in reply, retreating back over the front seat and into the back where he opened his writing tablet.

Samuel sat back there the remainder of the trip. The roads around the Salmon Hole were passable, he feeling the truck slide to the side only once. Ishmae was a good driver though, controlling the Model T without much effort. As they began ascending the steep hills he could hear the strain of the motor as the truck made its way. If they had taken the horse and buggy this part of the trip would take much longer he knew, as even the young mare his daddy kept would find the climb difficult.

As they neared the top Ishmae called to him. "Were almost there Samuel. Come up here and sit up front." Samuel climbed over the front seat. "Now listen, sometimes these folks can be a little funny. I've been coming up this way with doctor for almost fifteen years so folks know me pretty good. They don't notice the color of my skin. But if something is said or if something doesn't feel right don't you do or say nothing. Let me handle things. Alright?" said Ishmae in a manner that depicted the importance of the matter.

"Yes Sir. I understand. Some folks can be prejudice or just down right stubborn about some things." replied Samuel.

"That's right." said Ishmae. "It's no fault of theirs though. It's just how they were raised. Ignorance is handed down. My own momma taught me that. I tell ya what. After this, we take the long way back and stop off at the Tinkerville store."

Young Samuel's eyes got wider. "The good penny candy store? Deal!" Samuel exclaimed.

Ishmae paid his visit to the family he was suppose to see. A regular patient of Dr. Bugbee's he said. Old Mrs. Locke had been battling rheumatism for the past ten years or more and in the summer time with the heat and dampness from the rains it aches right on into her bones. Ishmae boiled up some indian gensing and gave it to her slowly, a little at a time. Leaving a pouch of the tea leaves he told her to drink a cup of tea before bed and in the afternoon if she needed. While he was inside, I waited outside, where I played with several other kids in a game of kickball on the back lawn.

As we left, I asked Ishmae if he preferred using the horse and buggy or the motor car.

"The motorcar Samuel. Without question. I know you like to take the reins on the buggy and you are partial to that horse but when the horse can't carry that weight then you have to. I've carried my share of weight and I tell you I'm too old to carry anymore. No Samuel, this motorcar suits me just fine." Ishmae explained.

Samuel thought about that, not taking long to realize there was something more to his words then the simple question he asked.

7

Who You Are

"Father? Why do we visit Grammy?", I asked one day.

"Because she's your grandmother Sam. And she's my mom. And some days I miss her. So I want to see her." father replied.

I sat thinking about that for a moment. I was only but six years old then, but Daddy always said I was smarter and wiser than most my age.

"The same for Uncle Jopey? " I asked again.

"The same thing Sam. He's my brother. And some days I miss him too." he chuckled then added. "Some days."

The sun was beginning to set as Daddy and I sat in the straight back chairs on the porch. The hotel was quiet with only six guests. A big difference of the dozen or more that usually occupy during this time of month so we had the porch to ourselves. Daddy read the Littleton Courier and mumbled to himself about railroad strike in Boston that had stopped all northern routes. Only trains that came down from Canada were stopping at the depot in town. I could read a little. The word 'train' and I knew the word 'Boston' from all the pamphlets around the hotel lobby.

As the sun began to set over the tall pines of Remich Park this time with Daddy was my favorite. Just his presence, his alone, made me happy. We could sit and not talk, and often we would. Just sit. And look out. And wonder. Or dream. Or pass a day in slow moving moments, as though time itself was of no consequent. It allowed for conversations that might not have happened. Daddy said it was what porches were made for.

"I'm your only kid." I said matter-of-factually, as though the notion just struck me.

Daddy did not answer right away, but took some time, as though lost. His face seemed to say that. "Yes. Yes Sam you are." he finally said, taking a breath.

"Why?" I asked.

"Because the Good Lord took your mother to a better place to help do his work." was his reply.

I nodded at that. Slowly, more for his own acknowledgment that I had listened then for actual understanding.

After some time passed, Daddy turned to me. "Sam? Do you know what a promise is?" he asked.

"I do. It's like when you say you will do something and you do. Or maybe not to do something and you don't." I answered.

"That's right. Promise me Sam you will always remember your mother. Her name. Elizabeth." he said.

"Of course Daddy. She made me the best blueberry pancakes ever. And Ishmae tells me stories about her all the time." I replied.

He placed a hand on my shoulder then. "Good. That's good."

A few minutes passed, then he added then it was my turn to ask. "Daddy, who was your father? This question seemed to take him by surprise as he looked toward those tall pines with a noticable sigh. "Joseph. His name was Joseph William." This made me excited as I exclaimed. "Just like my name Daddy! Samuel Ishmael William" "Yes Samuel. Just like your name."

What happened to him? Why don't we visit him?" I asked.

"Because he died. When he was young. I was only a few months born." Daddy answered. Then, "Come with me." And Daddy led me inside, up the stairs, to the family sitting room on the second floor. Standing in front of the rocking chair I had always seen and sometimes played under he explained of its importance. "This rocking chair Samuel was given to your grandmother by my grandmother. She used it to rock her daughter, my mother. And grandma passed it down to your mother. You were the last baby to be rocked in it. Someday, if its Gods plan, your wife will rock your children in it. And down the line it will go."

I didn't know what to say and didn't really want to say anything by chance of spoiling Daddys story. I could tell it was special to him.

"Would you like to hear another family story? About my father? Your grandfather." he asked.

Sitting up quickly, "You know it. I like winter stories. Like the sled you told me about."

Daddy chuckled a bit at that. Well, this one is in the winter too but not so thrilling as a sled ride. Here. Climb up." he said as he sat in the rocking chair, lifting me to his lap. "This is about a last Christmas and it's special. Really special." he said.

"It snowed heavily the night before Christmas Eve. December twenty-third was cold, colder than expected even for a northern New England winter. Wind blown snow drifts billowed across the unpaved dirt road, piling up against the farm house to just above the window sills. Even with lamps the snow covering even the smallest of window light darkened the rooms of the house to a haunting grayness, casting shadows in the corners, creeping to where the Christmas tree would soon stand in the living room. It would be his last Christmas. He knew it. My grandmother knew it. His parents knew it, his children knew it. The oldest boys drove their carriages through the storm the previous afternoon, arriving way ahead of the cold, wind, and snow. His parents, my great-grandparents, "Old Joe" and Susie, arrived by sleigh driven by his two horses Ned and Molly.

The tree was cut out the back of the barn and dragged across the frozen pond to the house. The boys cut the limbs, shortening it's stature, shaping it to perfection, perhaps the best looking tree they ever had. The younger kids, my dad and his sister, aptly nicknamed "sister" by him and the rest of the family, made cut out decorations, chaining colored paper together and folded snowflakes with fancy designs. The older women busied themselves in the kitchen. Keeping the wood stove stoked with oak and birch, cut during the fall with all of our hands, baking the traditional pies, including his favorite, my grandmothers' apple pie with the cross-crossed crust, which, ironically, was my favorite as well; selecting the preserves from the well stocked shelves in the root cellar: green beans, peas, corn, carrots, of course yellow squash, acorn, and blue Hubbard; beets, radishes, and turnips. All taken out of the garden through the course of the summer and summers before.

That morning Ned and Molly were again hitched as a team and harnessed to the packing roller, where "Old Joe", despite being near 80 and against Susie's wishes, sat atop the wagon while his son "Jopey", Joe Jr. led the team down the road, one end to the other, packing the snow as packed as possible. All the men in the family worked for the road agents at different points in time, taking care of the roads around the mountainside, either widening, laying down gravel, digging drainage ditches, or limbing bush and trees.

That Christmas Eve was jubilant and jolly, to be both cliche and nostalgic. The boys brought cigars, while "Old Joe" brought a taste of the latest batch of dandelion wine. The younger kids sat around listening to old stories as the family laughed together about their lives. And as he stood posing with all those around him, his clothes a little looser than usual, his frame a little more gaunt than last year, his elation radiated to each and everyone who gathered around him. No need for tears on a Christmas Eve with such love and happiness. He ate apple pie, is mother's recipe. And we sang. For him. His name was Raymond."

Daddy took out the gold pocket watch he carried, opened it, and looked at the time. "Now, its time to wash up for dinner."

"Can I hold it?" I asked.

Daddy knew what I was talking about. Whenever he took out his watch he knew I had to hold it first before putting it away. He handed it to me and I just let it set in my hand feeling its weight.

"Will this be mine someday like the rocking chair?" I asked.

"Someday Samuel. Someday." he said.

8

The Sled

"Daddy. What is this?" Samuel asked.

"It's called a travois." his father replied.

"It's a sled?" came Samuel's next question.

"It's a sled. But it's called a travois. A kind of sled used in Alaska. I traded a bicycle when I was sixteen for it. To take my sister for a ride." his father said.

"Oh. It must be old." Samuel said, running his hand over the slim design.

"Not that old son." his father replied laughing. "Let's take it for a ride."

Samuel sat in his bedroom, at his desk, pencil in hand and tablet opened. He thought of his fathers sled that sat in the far corner of the carriage house, opposite his bicycle. He thought about the trip up the mountain with Ishame a few days before. What life must have been like living way up there, out of town, with only your brothers and sisters as friends, for miles and miles. And he thought about all the things kids did together, and things families did together, and special moments when mothers and daughters and fathers and sons would bond tightly. Glancing out his window from that third floor, he saw his own father out front of the hotel, the sloping hillside, and sledding in the winter. So he began the story.

I laid there staring at the wallpaper design depicting a sepia toned country road winding around bowing trees and split rail fences, a mere boy of twelve. The differences between staring out the bedroom window and that wallpaper scene were few, for they were really one in the same. The small bedroom which I called my own was typical in farmhouse nature, all except the french styled glass doors with sheer antique white curtains that offered just enough light for a small kid not to be overly afraid of the dark and just enough to see out into the living room, with Gram sitting in her chair knitting while watching television. A twin bed with quilt and pillow kept the night chill out, while opposite, a four drawer upright dresser with oil lamp atop and hand stitched scarf to keep the dust off; the far wall another dresser, longer, donning black and white framed photographs of people and places I did not know. In the corner, a half closed door to the adjoining bedroom. The sounds at night, outside the window, were ones filled with the nocturnal antics of forested creatures. During the Fall, black bears could be heard up and down the road side, with their jaw-dropping, woofs and low moans, calling to each other in their own way. Coons, too, were a part of their own orchestra, as the momentary silence was a part of the night with their whining, cooing and crying. Every now and then, the bay of a hound dog from up the road a bit.

I would fall asleep this way and awake the exact same. Only, the morning hours could be heard the rummaging in the kitchen and the smell of coffee with idle, quiet chatter between Gram and my mom, or Gram and my dad, or sometimes all three. Outside the occasional whoom of a passing car down the dusty, winding, back country road; a dog or two barking for their morning chow, and of course a multitude of birds of every kind, feeding in the feeders that lined the edges of the house. Those years of a quiet boys existence are marked with indelible ink. Ink that is written on a parchment, although yellowed and stained with the passing of the time, nevertheless reads as though it were only yesterday. When the scroll is unsheathed from it's protective case and when the scroll is unrolled so delicately, the lines of memories are anything but marred.

One morning, later in years, the boy thought and read in his mind's eye of one such winter, not so long ago.

That winter morning was mild compared to the past. Last night's storm came over the mountain hamlet with wind and blinding snow falling horizontally.

Throwing on his pair of touch, well worn winter boots, the boy opened the front door, down the steps of the adjacent woodshed, and out into the cold wind. He muttered something about dumb snowmobiles being crazy. With a bucket in hand he high stepped his way to the barn, where he fed the pigs the leftovers from supper, and tossed a little chicken feed to the cackling chickens who all nestled in their boxes.

Later, by mid morning, the snow had let up, with only occasional flakes falling. The boy's dad came in from the barn with an unusual childlike excitement. Most always in good spirits, his dad was this time bursting with an enthusiasm that left the boy in wonder and curiosity.

"Get your snow pants on. Let's go sledding.", he said.

The boy did. Once outside, leant against the well house, a long blue wooden sled stood.

"It's a travois. Just dug it out of the loft of the barn. I haven't used it since…sheeeshhh, it's been awhile.", his dad said.

The boy ran his hand down the side of it. The sled shows signs of its age from the peeling blue paint and rusty nail heads.

"I traded a bike I built for this sled when I was …sixteen or so.", stated his dad. "Sister and I used it a lot down Jopey's back pasture. Want to take it for a ride down the backside to Ogantz?", asked his dad.

"Whoa. Yeahhh. That'll be a heck of a ride. Long way back pulling it.", said the boy.

His dad brushed it off. "Ehhh, only two miles, just over. The sun is out, it's getting warmer."

The father and son team took turns pulling the sled to the back place, where apple picking was abundant in the fall. There, the roll of the land sloped downward for about a mile and a half, straight to Ogantz Camp.

"Alright. Front or back?", asked his dad.

The boy looked over the sled. The travois as it was called. The long part of the sled hooked to the short steering part.

"I'm not even sure how to steer this thing, so back.", the boy replied.

"Good. Neither do I. Climb on.", said the dad.

"Great.", the boy replied back, while wrapping his arms around his dad's shoulders.

His dad pushed off, rocked his body back and forth for momentum, and the sled became a force left to gravity's whim. Down and down and down it went, gaining speed, sloshing snow over it's occupants. Neither spoke, but for a few low groans or 'whoa's as the sled somehow navigated around the turns of the road, the boys dad leaning his body, the boy doing the same. As the speed continued to gain, the sled became more difficult to control until they were running on one runner around the curves and embankments. Suddenly, it tipped, riding over the embankment, up and over into the woods, missing small trees by inches, until the roll over stopped them for good, burying themselves to their necks in cold wintry fluff.

"Jesus Christ.", the boy shouted.

His dad couldn't stop laughing. "That was great. Look at you!"

The boy took off his mitten wiping snow off his face. "That was….that was fast.", the boy replied in excited glee.

"The old sled can still move.",said his father.

"That's the fastest I've ever gone on a sled. Not even at Remich Park could I get that fast.", the boy replied.

"We best get out of this snow bank before we both freeze."

Together they pulled and heaved the sled back up to the packed down roadway.

"The rest of the way?", the dad asked.

"You bet!"the boy said back, this time he was taking the controls in the front.

Pushing off again, father and son made it to the bottom of the mountainside, finishing the ride. It would be many years later before the boy realized the significance of that one moment. After major life events had passed between the boy and his dad, it was not lost on him that that ride, although the last sled ride they would take, was only one the two would take together. Their vehicle would be one set in identical personalities as they both navigated the travesties of their lives. Their destination is ultimately different in nature but places recognized in importance. For despite their time together falling short, the sled to this day sets in the boys home, tucked in a corner, preserved and relished as a moment he took the ride of his life, awaiting another.

9

A Mother's Gift

"What was she like Ishmae? I mean, what was she really like?" Samuel asked as he and Ishmae walked along the railroad tracks that ran through town. He enjoyed his time with the man who was like family. He was someone he had always known. From the very beginning. And listening to his father and hearing stories from other people around town, Ishmae had been a part of the town for a long time. Everyone knew him and knew he was Dr. Bugbee's assistant when folks got ill. He was the person who was called on when the doctor was out of town. And for the last twelve years he was the one his father relied on for helping to keep the hotel from falling apart. Helping to keep him from falling apart. Ishmae became Samuel's confidante and closest friend. He knew his mother. Had a deep friendship with her that went beyond just a hired hand. Somehow, in some way, the two of them made a powerful and deep connection. More than likely it was because he was the one who brought Samuel into the world, delivering him from his mother in the middle of the living room of the hotel itself. And now, ten years later from that birthing day and nine years since his mother's departure from this world he too knew of that connection, for it took shape and grew in strength each and every day.

"Your mother? Your'e talking about your mother?" asked Ishmae, to be sure he heard the boy right.

Samuel nodded. "Hmm Mmm. Yes. Momma. What was she like?" he asked again.

"She was the most gentle and kindly lady I ever knew. My momma could yell in a flock of hens from the coop with a voice as loud as thunder. But your momma, she was a different kind. She was a giver. She gave folks things. Whether it was something made, like the pickle recipe I make, that was her own you know, or just sitting for a while and listening and talking cause she knew folks just wanted to be heard." Ishmae answered. "She understood the loneliness some folks feel."

Samuel sat there taking that in. "I miss her." he finally replied.

They continued walking along the rail, concentrating on just one step at a time. The rusted, iron rail was almost a perfect fit under their feet; his own arms outstretched for balance. Ishame on one side and he on the other, youth and old age in complete and perfect juxtaposition, set to the same pace and balance. As they neared the town center, Samuel jumped off the rail to walk the rest of the way.

"I can see the hotel." Samuel said as he gazed out over the rooftops, easily finding the hillside where his family's hotel stood.

"We get back, we'll get ourselves a piece of that apple pie that Miss Edith made this morning," said Ishmae.

Samuel's face lit up. "Deal."

"I miss her." Samuel said for the second time that day. They were sitting on the front porch, both with a plate of apple pie.

"Wait here." returned Ishame.

He came back not long afterwards. He had something in his hand. It was draped or covered by an old afghan blanket.

"Here. It's yours." Ishmae replied.

Samuel looked at the blanket and whatever the object was underneath. "What is it?" he asked.

"Take it. See." Ishmae said.

Samuel took it, holding it in his lap. "Its from your mother." Ishmae told him.

He looked up to the old man, his jaw almost dropping.

"But how…." he trailed off for a moment. "I mean,she's been gone for…for…" his voice faded.

"Samuel. This was your mothers. When she was a little girl. It's one of her most prized possessions and she trusted me to take care of it for her until I could give it to you. I'm letting you see and hold it now, but I'll keep it. Until you have a daughter. It's who she wanted it to go to. That was her wish and the promise I made to her."

Samuel unwrapped it from the covered blanket, holding it, staring at the doll. He ran his finger over the doll's hair, traced the pattern of its dress. "She…my momma held this? This was hers? When she was little?" Samuel asked, his voice beginning to waver.

"She did. And it will be yours to give to your daughter some day." said Ishame.

Samuel could feel his eyes getting wet, reddening, as his breaths came in short, sobbing gasps. Laying his head on Ishmae's shoulder the older man held him close.

"It'll be alright. Your momma is here, and I'm here too. I won't ever be too far. And this doll here. Will be kept safe until you are ready to receive it."

Samuel nodded. Understanding. He brushed the doll's hair with a caress and held it like fragile china. He studied the doll's face for a time then whispered to it. "I miss you momma."

10

New to Town

That spring a new family moved to town. Recognizing the need for more assistance, doctor Bugbee wrote to colleagues in Chicago inquiring about the re-location of any doctor who was willing and able to make his way to a small mountain town in New Hampshire, calling it home. To his surprise, he got no response. Also to his surprise, a new family moved to town not long after. Dr. Frank Thompson with his daughter Mary. Dr. Thompson was a widower of four years. Raising his only daughter on his own, she was the perfect image of her well versed and charming mother, to which he knew raising her on his own in Lynn, Massachusetts may not be in her best interest, especially considering she nearing her teenage and more impressionable years. Having gone to medical school in Boston he knew of the gentleness of New England particularly the further northern parts. Climbing aboard the Boston and Maine heading north, he and Mary rode until the feeling felt right to depart.

After a weeks stay at the Thayers Hotel, Dr. Thompson purchased property on South Street, at the corner of Bronson Street. A grand old style Victorian with a large barn for the motorcar and stalls for a carriage and a team to pull it if he wanted. Mary loved the house the first moment she saw it especially the barn and loft where she became mother to baby chickens, rabbits, and even a goat later on.

"Daddy. Can I have the bedroom at the top? It overlooks the entire town." she said excitedly.

"You won't be afraid being up there all on your own?" he asked.

"Daddy. I'm almost fourteen years old. I don't get scared of the dark anymore." Mary replied.

"Oh, well, pardon me. I suppose you can then." her father said with a smile and laugh.

As the new school year approached the new girl in town began making friends in the neighborhood. South Street had an abundance of families with children. With large front and back yards, the woods at the bottom of Mount Eustis, the Ammonoosuc River a stones toss away, and Main Street a short walk and skip down over the hill, there was enough to keep the kids busy and entertained. As Mary explored her new surroundings, she made a close friendship with Cynthia, the daughter of parents Louisa and Edward. Her mother was a seamstress and her father worked for the railroad. Cynthia introduced Mary to all of her friends, together and sometimes with others, showing Mary all the highlights of town. Mary found herself really liking the river and all the dams that aligned the banks from Apthorp to the Saranac Glove Factory. She and her new friends really liked going to the footbridge, making it swing to and fro. The first time Mary was frightened, no doubt about it, but the more she did it, the more thrilling it became. Swimming in the river itself was always good for a full day, as long as she promised not to go near the dams, above or below. The tall standing pines on High Street became a destination just before the end of summer, a few days before school started again. A small gazebo became a meeting place for her and her friends to gather, laugh, and play. Particularly fun, was imagining all the guests that would motorcar up the road to the large hotel at the top. What lives did they live? Where did they live and why did they come here? She and her girlfriends would take turns inventing stories.

When school started, she began the sixth grade. Littleton school was small, much smaller than the elementary school she attended in Philadelphia. There she sat in a class of thirty-eight other students! Here she was one of only fifteen. She liked the smaller class size and was fond of her teacher too. Mr. Smith was kind and fair but strict with the boys when he needed to be.

Having shoulder length raven black hair and a fair complexion Mary stood out from the other girls, who were more typically French and English descent with a little Irish tossed in for good measure. Blonde, brunette, and red haired students were of the abundance. Nevertheless, kids began asking her all kinds of questions about city living, what Philadelphia was like, did she know famous people, and of course what the boys were like there. Her answers ranged from 'it's horrible', 'lots of brick buildings', and 'no she didn't' other than her mother who was an active supporter of the woman's suffrage movement.

Going to school in the small mountain school was not difficult. She enjoyed her classes and made friends quite easily. Walking to school from her new home on South Street she particularly enjoyed crossing over the bridge that ran across the river each morning. Some mornings the fog would lift off the rushing waters that flowed over the dam at the grist mill making for a really pretty view. The early morning folks would be just opening their doors to their stores along Main Street and other kids would meet up and walk to school together. Mary was no different. It wasn't long before she met Doria, Dolores, with smaller sisters Irene and Sandra, who lived at the corner of Elm Street and Main. Dolores was her age, Doria a little older, and Irene only six years old, in the first grade. Sandra who tagged along holding Irene's hand was only four. Usually she would meet them in the center of town at the Carnegie Library, but every now and then they would walk all the way down to the bridge where the four of them would watch the fog roll off from the river below.

"It sure is beautiful in the morning isn't it?" said Dolores.

"Almost like steam from a tea kettle." replied Mary.

"We best be leaving or we'll be late. Come along now." insisted Doria, the older and always motherly sister.

Taking little Irene's hand, the three sisters turned back toward the direction of the school. Mary lingered just a moment longer however. Peering down over the railing of the bridge, she caught sight of a boy. Looking away and rubbing her eyes, she looked back, and sure enough, he was there. Just sitting on a rock, with a stick, poking at the water. Doria turned back just then.

"Mary. Come along now. We'll be late." she shouted.

"There's a kid down there. On a rock. Just sitting." Mary stated.

"Oh. I saw him. That's just Samuel. He's probably waiting for his Daddy at the mercantile. Now come on." Doria said.

"You on along. I'll catch up." Mary replied.

Doria and Dolores both rolled their eyes, holding Irene's and Sandra's hand, picking up their pace.

Mary peered down over the rail again.

"Hey. You down there." she yelled down.

The boy didn't hear at her so she yelled down louder.

"Hey. You. Boy on the rock." she yelled again.

This time he did hear her and looked up. He didn't wave but only gazed back to her for what seemed like a long time then slowly got up, hopping across the rocks and up over the embankment. Mary walked back across the bridge to the other side where they met almost at the same time.

"Hi." the boy said to her as he made his way back up to the street level.

"Hi." Mary replied back. "What were you doing down there?" she asked.

"Nothing. I just sometimes wait there for my Daddy when he's picking up packages over there at the depot store." he said.

Mary looked over at the long building that stood along side the railroad tracks. Being across from the train depot, the daily train that ran through town would disembark passengers at the depot and unload crates and such at the depot store, mostly farming equipment and bags of grain and seed.

"Oh. I walk across the bridge every morning going to school. This is the first time I've seen you." she replied in return.

"It's not everyday. Only when Ishmae isn't available to pick things up." he said.

"My name is Mary. What's yours?" she asked.

"Samuel. Samuel Anderson. I live up that way. At the Chiswick Inn on top of the hill." he replied.

33

I know of it. My Daddy is a doctor he went there when we were only three days newly arrived to see a someone who was ill. I waited on the porch for him. It sure is big and fancy." she said.

"Hey. I remember that day. It was Saturday. My bedroom is on the third floor and I saw you and him drive up in the buggy." he said.

The two kids just stood there for quite sometime without saying another word, as though all they had to say had been said. When Mary broke the silence it was at the same exact time as when a cloud of fog rose above the bridge. They both simultaneously moved their hands through the wispy billows of cloud.

"Wow. I've never seen it do that before." Samuel said in an astonished and amazed tone of voice.

"It's beautiful." Mary replied moving her fingers slowly, like dancing in a dream. "It's like a dream."

"Samuel? Samuel!" came a shout from up the street. Samuel turned to look over his shoulder to see his Daddy standing at the tracks waving for him to come along.

"I best be going. I'll see you at school later. Maybe we can come back this afternoon?" Samuel asked her.

"I would like that. See you at school." Mary replied.

As she turned and walked away, Samuel uttered the phrase for the first time in his life that he didn't know then would become more common. "Sure is beautiful in the morning."

11

The Music Man

On any given day soft rat-a-tat-rat's could be heard across town. Somewhere distant 'the music man' as he was known, was tapping on his drum, holding a concert all on his own for whomever wished to listen. Finding tucked away corners around the outskirts of main street, his audience listened from a distance and up close. The music man was a different kind of person. A loner. A person of solitary comforts. One who wished not the notoriety or companionship by many. But he sure loved his drum. And those synchronized and patterned taps he made with his sticks reverberated up and down and across the river, bending ones ear to listen a little harder. His name was Peter and he rode his bicycle all over town. He was nineteen and his family came from down the road, a couple of towns over. It was said his grandparents came from a tiny farming community nestled high up on the ridge lines. And it was also said Peter had the love of music in his veins and the gift of voice in his heart. He was my cousin, years older. My father's brothers' son. He carried two drum sticks. Always. No matter where he went. Sometimes he would sit outside the library downtown and just play and sing. Folks would stop, nod, smile, and say things like 'that's real nice' and 'come play in our choir next week'. Sometimes he did. The music he made came directly from his Soul and was meant to be shared when the time called for it and when it struck him hard not by a designated time slot.

As I sat at my desk on an evening during late fall, notepad and ink pot and quill in hand, I thought about my cousin and me and the gift he would sometimes share with our town.

"The young man was always in tune, on each beat, that he heard so keenly, spiritually, physically. His quest for a perfect beat, an unwavering rhythm, a drum roll of explosion that left sticks to anything that would make sound wherever he went. He was of a different breed. A cloth cut from a fabric so finely and tightly woven, each stitch was unique only to himself.

For the wanderlust for music was in his blood, handed down to him from great grandparents and beyond in search of a happiness that perked his ears to a silence of sound. The meeting of people, their stories, their music, their very lives, how they lived and how they loved, enthralled every part of him; electrified his blood, urged him on, a motivation that became a relentless quest for his own perfection. So with a bag slung across shoulders that were squared and strong with determination, he took on the illusion of the traveling bard by family and friends without even knowing it. He would often join community bands, setting the beat for the music at gazebo concerts in the park, or parades, or social events at the many large hotels. Anywhere he could bring his drum and there was a need."

12

Mischevous

The class assignment that day was to rewrite five different paragraphs from the English text book, using proper sentences, like periods and capital letters and fixing run-on sentences. As he sat in the middle of the room, barely through the first paragraph, he looked about at his classmates, their eyes fixed downward, soft scratching from pencils busy and at work. Taking a side glance up, he could see the teacher, Mr. Edwards, sitting behind the solid oak desk, book in hand, studiously reading its contents. His mind was not on the assignment but the annual kite flying contest in a couple of weeks. He had been participating for the last three years. The first year was miserable, his kite actually falling apart in mid air, fluttering its way to the ground, embarrassment written all over his face. The second year, a little better, with better design and materials, but still no match for the senior high school students who studied the lay of physics, aerodynamics, and wind currents. This year though, was all his. He was determined to win and win with a box kite of his own design, first prize being four tickets to the cinema. Four tickets made four films. He loved going to the cinema shows. However, as of late, every now and then, he began thinking perhaps it would be nice to go with a friend, reducing four down to only two shows. It surprised him that he didn't mind the thought of that notion.

But first he needed to make it through the next twenty five minutes of English class with Mr. Edwards, with two paragraphs left to write. It felt daunting and impossible. Just then the classroom door opened, principal Smith walking in with his usual pompous aire and attitude in his gait. Moving quickly and purposefully across the room, he went directly to Mr. Edwards where he lowered himself, whispering low. Right away, deep concern furrowed Mr. Edwards brow. Looking up he gazed past the other students directly to Samuel where he tried to pretend he was fully immersed in the assignment.

"Mr. Anderson? Excuse me Mr. Anderson. Approach my desk please.", said Mr. Edwards.

Samuel caught his attention, immediately rising from his seat, moving past his classmates where their attention was broken also, now directed to the front of the room. Standing in front of his teacher, "Yes Sir?", he answered.

"Go directly to Principal Smith's office. Sit outside his door, and wait for him there. Do not go anywhere else. Wait.", Mr. Edwards sternly directed.

Samuel hesitated a moment, an obvious nervousness suddenly overtaking him. "Yes sir. Yes sir.", stepping unsurely across the classroom and out into the hallway, while he knew his classmates were watching him every step of the way. Once in the hallway and before he closed the door behind him, he heard Mr. Edwards voice, "Back to work class. No concern of yours."

With sandy brown hair and fine chiseled features, Samuel looked well above his fifteen years of age. His older brother John, four years older, was often mistaken for the youngest of the two. He sat outside Principals Smith as directed, quietly and feeling alone, like the whole world was watching him and wondering what crime he had committed. The school secretary, Mrs. Green, busied herself with various degrees of paperwork. From folding, bending, stuffing envelopes, scribbling signatures, checking boxes, and placing information in teacher's mailboxes, she paid absolute no nevermind to Samuel. He could have been invisible.

"Mr. Anderson, follow me.", Mr. Smith's voice woke Samuel from a half daze. Quickly standing, Samuel followed him into his office where Mr. Smith closed the door.

"Sit down Mr. Anderson.", as Mr. Smith made his way behind his desk. Seating himself, he opened a folder, reading it's contents.

"Now Mr. Anderson, can you tell me what you know about Mr. Sullivan?", asked his principal.

"Sullivan sir?, replied Samuel. "I'm not sure…"

"Mr. Anderson, you know him. I know him. And I know that you know that I know him. So just say you know him son.", said his principal as his eyes seemed to gaze a hole right through him.

"I know him", replied Samuel, the only thing he could say.

"Good. That's a start. Now Mr. Anderson, what did you and Mr. Sullivan do together last Friday night?"principal Smith asked.

Samuel stood silent for a moment, not at all comfortable in the moment, feeling a lot like he did the last time his father confronted him with the lie he told about not mowing over the widow Mosely's flower bed. This time would be different. Possibly even worse.

13

Being Young

"I hope Daddy doesn't make string beans tonight for dinner. I hate string beans", said Mary.

"Why don't you like them?", asked Samuel.

"Because Daddy doesn't cut off the ends and the little string nibs get caught in my teeth,'' she replied.

As the sun sank ending the summer day, the two teenage kids sat on the covered, wrap-around Victorian porch, he, Samuel, working on putting together a box kite, and she, Mary, drawing in a sketch pad she had gotten last Christmas. It was half filled. Mary Thompson loved to draw but the fancy came and went at will. She had some talent, easily recognizing and visualizing how curves and lines come together to create an image. And she could have been much better if she would only practice everyday, but that wasn't her way at all. There were too many other things to explore and occupy one's time. Like boys. And one particular boy who sat in front of her now.

A young lady raised to play the piano when she was six years old, needlepoint at eight, helping with the fall canning with her mother and aunts who lived in the next county over on a small farm that provided local vegetables to the many stores, Mary was of dark complexion, with rounded cheeks and dark hair, dark round eyes that glowed with the radiance of her youth. At sixteen she was maturing into adult womanhood, leaving at least her Daddy a little concerned. Her father was busy mostly, paying more attention to the sick and ailing than he did to his own family. At least that's how it seemed. She looked the part of a young lady in waiting when she took the time to properly brush her hair and adorn herself in the fashionable dress, complete with buckled shoes and stockings. But she felt much more comfortable when wearing the very feminist slacks and buttoned shirt, not exactly figure flattering, but all the rage among the national women's rights movements across the country. Her Daddy approved, although with a little reluctance, as it not only covered her blossoming womanhood but also gave her a sense of pride that his little girl would be an independent young woman dependent on no man's wealth, fortune, or fame. Mary would make her way in the world on her own merit. Thank you very much. And she would follow in her Daddy's footsteps to attend medical school for nursing.

"Eeeeee, I can see what you mean.", Samuel replied back, glancing only briefly in her direction. "I prefer corn on the cob myself."

If the two had grown up together ever since they could walk the closeness they shared would certainly make sense. And if their families had lived next to one another on a quiet, dirt road street, in a quiet neighborhood consisting of upscale Victorian homes built specially for doctors, lawyers, business owners, railroad tycoons, and captains of industry, that would certainly make sense. But Mary's father was newly arrived to town, moving here only last month because old Dr. Beebe was in need of help and couldn't keep up with the growing town and the number of folks who needed to see him each month. Her father enjoyed telling folks about how he had met her mother at a church supper, asking her out to the church dance the very next weekend; married after a proper courtship and length of respectable time. And because of this, he needed to move he and his daughter as far away as possible. Coming from Massachusetts, he chose northern New Hampshire, not because he had ever visited or known anyone, but because the train from Boston went in that direction. The constant telling and re-telling of his marriage, of his wife, of her death, to everyone that offered their condolences, it became too much. He needed to find a place for he and his daughter where nobody knew them.

As the sun sank behind the oak tree in the front yard, the shadows of the rooftops became less and less and the steady humming of the crickets more noticeable from the pond at the end of the road. Evening chirpers her grandma called them. Mary's eyes lifted up to watch Samuel build the kite. He was cute. Short, sandy brown hair with equally light brown eyes, with a face that resembled the Greek boys she had seen in Life magazine and her school text books. He dressed rather shabbily, his shirt un-tucked and his shoes untied most of the time. Known for getting into scruff matches in the schoolyard, he wasn't considered a school bully, but he wasn't considered a good homework mate either. But it wasn't about his style of dress that she realized she liked, or even admired, it was the way he would listen to her and give that smile he had every time she said something in a funny way. A small laugh not meant to be sarcastic or insulting, but genuine and sincere, like a friend gives to a friend to make them smile in return. Not to mention of course he loved horses. Almost as much as she did.

Turning her attention back to her drawing, she made one more small etch, put her charcoal pencil down, and held up the drawing pad.

"There. What do you think?", she said as she peered at him.

Samuel lifted his eyes briefly, seeing the sketch but not really looking at it, as his hands were busy holding two pieces of balsa wood while his elbow struggled to press the rice paper in place against the thin pieces of frame. Again, he only looked up briefly, enough to pass a glance, before he lowered his attention back to the kite. But then, quite unusually, he stopped what he was doing, actually dropping the framework of the kite, causing the rice paper to flutter aside and the kite to collapse. He caught Mary's eyes, holding them for what seemed like enough time to lapse to rush out of his teens and into independence. As she sat holding up the small drawing she caught his look. One not complimentary of her work, but something more. It was difficult to describe. As the single bulb from the porch glowed brighter as the night sky turned darker, the two kids who grew up together no longer were the same that ran around their yards chasing each other and snatching cookies before dinner, but like magic they realized there was possibly something more to their friendship.

"Mary, time to come in dear. Say goodnight to Samuel.", came the voice of her father from the dining room window, which stayed cracked open just enough to overhear the two young people's voices.

"Be right there Daddy.", she declared back. Their eyes still stuck on the other, she moved ever so slightly to break whatever spell they both suddenly came afflicted with. "Good night Samuel. It's been a nice night together. And, …I hope you get your kite working.", she giggled, eyeing it in a dismantled heap on the table, just enough to make him smile.

After some hesitation, perhaps gasping for what to say, "Thanks Mary. Maybe after I get it made we can fly it together. Up on top of Park Hill, by the hotel. That's where I live." Samuel replied.

"I'd really like that.", Mary said in return, picking up her sketchpad and pencils, slowly moving past him. As a young gentleman raised with manners, he quickly came to his feet, reaching and fumbling for the front door latch, opening it for her. They didn't need to say anything else as he watched her enter her home and he softly closed the door. Samuel stepped off the porch, stumbling as he misstepped the last step. Taking one last look over his shoulder, he mumbled, "My kite.", and scurried back to the porch to retrieve it.

Mary climbed the stairs to the second floor, skipping the first couple, her hand quickly sliding up the curvaceous banister, entering her bedroom and closing the door behind her. Placing the sketch she had just made carefully on her dressing table, she studied it one more time. The horse she drew she could have drawn in the dark with a blindfold. Horseback riding since she was ten years old, the last six years saw her become an accomplished equestrian, competing in events held at the Mt. Washington Hotel when she and her parents would visit. Her horse, "Shadow, was her most beloved companion and she wouldn't know what to do without him. She picked up the sketch, sliding the corner under the beveled edge of the vanity mirror along with two dozen other sketches of Shadow.

14

First Kiss

The early evening light was just leaving and the coolness of the air was setting comfortably. The perfect time for kite flying with just the right weather. The air currents were not as dense and humid during the late afternoons, allowing for better altitudes and less drag on the kite. All the books Samuel had been reading on aviation and flying held true for kites as well. In fact, it was what he was doing his science project on this year. With the new bi-planes being used in Europe as well as for agriculture, like crop dusting, he was pretty certain where his future was heading.

The hillside which the hotel sat upon was empty of people, allowing not just privacy but a good runway for takeoff. Mary arrived on time, with two of her girlfriends, Doria and Dolores, with their little sister Irene in tow. Samuel was thrilled to see her, with a little less enthusiastic towards the others. Still, though, she came, which meant something to him and not just words.

"Hi Samuel. I'm here. I mean, we're here. You remember my girlfriends? We met at the bridge that morning. Doria and Dolores. And their little sister Irene. Daddy wouldn't let me come unless we all came together." Mary told him.

"Oh. Yes. Yes, of course I do. Good to see you again girls. Have you ever flown a kite before?" Samuel asked looking from one to the other.

"I have." said Doria.

"We haven't." replied Dolores, pointing to little Irene too.

"Well. It's really easy. As your sister can tell you. But unless you understand the mechanics of why the kite actually fly's its just a kids toy. Now, this kite right here. I built myself. With aerodynamics kept in mind." Samuel rattled on.

"I know about why kites fly. I've studied about flying. I want to be an aviator someday." Doria said interrupting, with a rather smug tone, not meant to be outdone.

"Oh. I see. Well, then…" Samuel started to say then drifted off.

"Well, I can't wait to see you fly it Samuel. I've been waiting for three whole days." Mary chimed in hoping to break the ice.

"Alright. Well, first you…you hold this ball of string Mary. I'll hold the kite up. When I say go, you run as fast as you can. I'll let go, and she'll fly high." Samuel replied excitedly.

Mary nodded, taking the large ball of string. "There's enough string here to reach the moon!" she said with a high pitch.

"Not quite that much, but it will fly over downtown I bet." Samuel replied. "Ok. Ready? Go."

Mary began running while the other girls watched on. She ran down the hill a bit, then across, then back down a little more. She felt when Samuel let go and as she looked over her shoulder, the kite was surely flying.

"Let out a little string!" Samuel shouted.

Mary unwound some string, stopping now, as the kite caught the lower wind currents gaining altitude. "It's flying!" Mary shouted back.

"Of course. I built it. And you're a great pilot." Samuel said in return loudly.

Just then a voice came from the front porch. "If any of you kids would like ice cream, there's some left from the social tonight. Come up to the porch to get it." said Ishmae leaning over the porch rail watching the kite in the sky.

The three sisters didn't hesitate. "We'll see you two later. Have fun with your kite."

Samuel walked down the hill to where Mary stood, letting out more string, as the kite called for it. Seeing Samuel standing next to her she moved a little closer to him. "This is fun Samuel. Thank you."

"I'm glad you came Mary. And glad you like it. I think I want to be a pilot someday. I can understand why Doria wants to be one too." Samuel said.

"If I close my eyes, I can imagine myself small, sitting up there, on that kite, looking down on everyone and everything. Just feeling the wind against me and riding on the air like a feather." Mary said in a dream like state.

Hearing her words, watching her subtle movements, how the fading light of the sky set against her dark, raven hair; her fingers sliding along the string delicately, he felt as though he was the wind that moved her and how lucky he would be to move like the wind against her so. He said low, "I'm jealous of the wind."

"What's that?" asked Mary, fully concentrating on the kite above them.

"Just how lucky the wind is." he replied.

Mary stopped, looking to him. And then, at that moment, both their lives changed. Laying his hand on hers that held the string ball, their eyes locked in a timely rhythm with their own breath, as they both leaned closer, their lips touching for the first time. He could feel her nervousness, her body trembling. Parting he asked, "You alright?"

She nodded, not really sure if she was or not, but not wanting the moment to stop. "I think so. Don't stop." And with that he kissed her again, this time their lips moving together, like the wind against the kite, high above, as though on the same current.

15

Coming of Age

"Thinking of taking a swim?", asked Samuel.

Mary startled, turning to see him approaching, both hands in his pockets, as was accustomed to his posture, one that spoke of a casual and carefree, young candor.

"You are a terrible boy Samuel for scaring me like that.", Mary replied. "But yes. Yes I was. Of our summer fun on the rocks down there. Swimming in the river with friends. It was a short summer."

Samuel placed his arm lightly around her shoulder. That summer was their last year of high school. The only school they had ever known, sitting high on the hillside overlooking the town. Growing up at the hotel his family owned and managed, he would wake each morning, dress in his third floor bedroom, crash down to the first floor, grabbing a slice of hot buttered and jam toast along the way, to stop at the front porch, looking out across to the next hill where the school stood. The sun would barely be peeking when he descended the front steps, counting each one of his own in long, hurried strides down to Main Street and across the very same bridge where they each stood now, to tap on the front door of Mary's home tucked up behind the train depot. Her father would answer, dressed in his doctor's finest. Shouting over his shoulder the request for her presence was the same each and every time. "Mary! Samuel is here. On time as always."

"It was. Some summers are like that I suppose. I suppose the older you get the shorter they become. It just means we ain't kids anymore Mary. You'll be starting nursing school soon in Massachusetts and I'll be leaving too I suppose. Father wants me to pursue education in business. He says the hotel will be mine someday and it will take more than just his knowledge to run it properly. Times are changing, he says." said Samuel, his arm sliding from her shoulders where his hand found her own, entwining fingers like they what seemed a thousand times before.

Mary placed her head on his shoulders. It was as though they had always known one another. Almost from the beginning, when she and her daddy arrived in the small mountain town. Samuel was the first kid she met. Right here on this bridge. He and his father were picking up sacks of grain from the feed store across the tracks. While his father began in engaging in discussion on the topic of economic commerce through the use of twice weekly passenger trains north, one that a ten year old little boy found not at all interesting, he walked down to the bridge, where he would often scramble across the rocks underneath to look for trapped fishes in the pools of water. On that day though, he didn't go under the bridge, but saw the raven haired little girl eyeing the flowing water down below. And his first words to her were "Thinking of taking a swim?"

Mary listened to him, her eyes fixated and starry on the rushing water. "I know Samuel. I know." she replied.

"Then what is it?", asked Samuel.

"We won't be seeing each other for a whole year." she said with a tremble in her voice.

Their hands squeezed instinctively.

"True. True. But remember. You're my girl. And I love you. And we are always better together than apart." Samuel told her, kissing her cheek. Just like that, her voice stopped faltering at the nervousness of the future, and, unbeknownst to her, her body as well.

16

Finding Mary

The yellow, morning light reflected off from each swaying bough outside the boys window. He sat writing in his journal as he did this time each morning, each morning being the solitude which nurtured his thoughts, sowing those onto the lines of the page. Through the splay of branches blue sky emerged with the occasional wings in flight, flirting on the air currents. Crisp, fall air conditioned his bedroom high on the third floor. He chose this room when only fourteen years old, his parents thinking it was too far removed from the family, but that was the point. He enjoyed the quiet and he relished being alone. Alone, he could create entire worlds and characters who lived in those worlds without distractions. He loved the feel of the pencil on paper; the soft etching as each curlicue of handwriting became legible. And in that legibility he most always gained a clearer understanding. An acknowledgment, that even from an early age, he knew he was a little different from other young men. Where they dreamed of chasing planes, trains, and girls, he had other ambitions. His passion lied in the written word and how his words in particular could possibly influence and change entire philosophies. A bold task he knew.

But this morning it was not those dreams that kept him from his concentration but the girl who had recently been keeping him awake at night. Raven haired, slight of build; first appearance a fragile beauty. Seldom did she reveal the deep down strength she possessed but when she did it was like a hurricane wind that whirls its swirling force. A quick but swift action with lasting effects. With a wide smile and gleaming eyes that looked into your own, she was genuine and real. They began as best friends, almost from the very beginning. A platonic relationship that was built in teasing fun, adventures, laughter and mutual understanding. Distancing from the other when needed, returning when wanted. But even at a young age their lives were complicated. Both new graduates, he was expected to carry on the male lineage of military training and she to attend teaching school, like her mother and grandmother before. He came from a degree of wealth, the hotel which he lived high on the hillside built by his great grandfather after the war; she from a hard working family, her father a doctor, and her mother, before she died, a nurse; where wealth was measured in gratefulness for what you had and not things given to you that are not needed. Yet an undeniable attraction was there. Like an unspoken sonnet verse, they both knew and felt it.

Despite the intricacies of their families, they gained more being together than apart. She felt comfortable with him shedding a tear, and he went back to her to dry such tears with words of kindness and encouragement. In time, with a gentle hand to make them disappear. So their lives were created one step at a time. On walks they took, short or long, but with solid contentment of just being there. And when the last step was taken, it was like an unmentioned sigh of despair. Early evenings would cast out its last light, leaving them in a solitary affair once again.

He imagined her thinking of him. Half scoffing at such a notion, knowing that his thoughts were caught between wishful thinking and fantasy. Yet his imagination took them places. Creating fictitious characters portraying his own sentiments. Revealing emotions that could make him seem foolish. Yet, as a writer he felt worth the risk. The image of her hung like an apparition, so real he was sure he could reach out and touch her. Sometimes he would even try. A small laugh then as the figment faded.

And so it was. Through brief yet meaningful interludes to longer well spent journeys, exploring new places for the first time, or old places for the first time together. They were happy. A picture of holding hands, an arm around the other, a kiss in an intimate and private moment, unforgettable; was less than important then just the satisfaction of being together. To say he yearned for something more would be true. To say he wished not to cloud what they already had would also be true. For their energy was undeniable. Like a raging river, not easily navigated, fraught with swirling waters, frigid and deep, their feelings were strong, passionate, and, if tested, one of wild abandonment the other had never known.

17

The Ring

"Mary, Mary, what on earth is wrong? What's going on?", Samuel asked her.

Mary sobbed in near hysterics while pacing back and forth around the gazebo, up and down stairs, walking in circles around it.

"I lost it Samuel. I lost my grandmother's ring. I've looked, and looked, and it's ….it's gone." Mary replied in deep wails and sobs.

As he watched her, he couldn't help but want to help. Mary and he had become best friends together since the first time they saw each other. When she moved to town with her father up on South Street, he would stop by her house to deliver groceries for her father and of course glance about trying to see her. Working for the market on main street had it's advantages to which delivering groceries to the new girl in town quickly became one of them.

"Think hard Mary. Where was the last time you saw it?", Samuel asked calmly.

"The day before yesterday. I was at Thayers' with Daddy helping him with a lady who had fallen ill. I had it then. It must have slipped from my finger when I was filling a basin with water." Mary said.

"Has that happened before? Slipped from your finger I mean." inquired Samuel.

"Once. Once before. But that was at home. It was easy to find then." replied Mary.

Taking both her hands in consolation, Mary's sobs began to decrease in frenzy.

"You go back home. Look everywhere. Not once or twice, but look everywhere three times. I'll go to Thayer's Hotel and look around there. We'll find it Mary. You did before." said Samuel.

Mary nodded, took a deep breath, turned and left in the direction of South Street and her home.

"Mister Edwards. Good day to you. I hope you are well. I'm here to ask if you by chance have found a pearl ring." asked Samuel.

"Ahhhh, Master Anderson, You have completed my English assignment I presume seeing you are out gallivanting around town looking for missing rings?" Mr. Edwards replied.

"Oh. Yes Sir. Last night sir. Four pages Sir. Mary lost her grandmother's ring. She thinks it may have slipped from her finger while helping her father with an ill patient here the other day." replied Samuel.

Mr. Edwards taught eleventh grade English classes at Littleton High School during the week, but on the weekends he helped out at the front desk at Thayers Hotel. Not because he really enjoyed it, every student at LHS knew Mr. Edwards really didn't like people especially kids, but everyone did know he was more than a little smitten with Gladys Bilodeau, head housekeeper.

"Yes. That would have been Mrs. Copenhaver." said Mr. Edwards as he turned his attention to the registry book. Flipping back a couple of pages he traced his finger down the list.

"Yes, yes. Mrs. Adeline Copenhaver. Traveling from Boston. Was suppose to stay two days then take the Boston and Maine up to Portland. She left this morning. It seems the mountain air didn't agree with her but I think it was the laudanum she was taking for her dizzy spells she said." he replied with a chuckle.

"Well, I'm sure Mary's dad helped her. But about the ring.", replied Samuel.

"Room 402. Upstairs, turn left. Two doors down. It's empty. As I recall Mary was helping her father."

"Yes. That's what she said. Thank you Mr. Edwards.", replied Samuel as he began stepping away but then turned back. "Ohhh, Mr. Edward? You're a great English teacher."

Samuel turned at a quick pace, reaching the grand staircase, skipping stairs to the second floor.

"Hmmmpf. We shall see about you Mr. Anderson. We shall see." muttered Mr. Edwards from behind the front desk.

Samuel found room 402 easy enough. As he opened the door stepping inside, he searched first the beside tables. On top, behind, and underneath, in the drawers, behind the curtains and under the bed. He was about to give up when he remembered Mary said filling up the wash basin. Walking across the hall to the bathroom, he entered and there it was. Sitting on the basin all neat and pretty. Picking it up, he gently slipped it into his shirt pocket skipping down the stairs as he came up.

"Found it Mr. Edwards. Thank you!" he cried out as he ran out the tall double front doors.

Knowing the shortest route to Mary's house on South Street, he ran down the back of Thayers, cutting down River Street, Saranac, and then across the footbridge that led up to South Street. Out of breath, he ran up on Mary's front porch knocking on the door. "Mary. Mary. It's me Samuel. Come here. Quick." Samuel yelled panting.

Opening the door, it was obvious she had been crying again.

"Samuel, I haven't found it anywhere…" she began then stopped suddenly, caught her breath, as Samuel held up her grandmothers pearl ring between his fingers.

"You found it!" Mary said in barely a whisper, wrapping her arms around him.

As his own arms held her Samuel knew then this was a moment to remember and that someday he would need to remember it and probably even write about.

18

Hand In Hand

Samuel arrived at Mary's house at the time she gave him; just after dinner, exactly seven o'clock. The walk from the hotel and down over the Pleasant Street hill was short enough and one he had made before since his Daddy first told him he was old enough to explore a little on his own. Lined with large homes with wrap around porches like the hotel, he had come to know almost everyone in the neighborhood. And they knew him and his Daddy well too. In a small town where everyone knows one another, when someone walks by your home, and you happen to be sitting on the porch, a friendly wave and a fond hello will always occur. Quite often an invitation to "come on up and sit and have something to drink" which, in itself is a right nice invite, but in reality one that was full of questions about who was staying in the big place up on the hotel, how long they would be there, and were they someone of recognition. Enough times like this, one comes to know ones neighbors quite well and has learned exactly how to articulate such answers so as not to give away to much information about the traveling guests and not too little to be invited up on the porch again another time. Nice folks with a curiosity that gets the best of them sometimes.

At the bottom of the hill and the center of town, adjacent to the Methodist Church, was the town watering trough for the livestock. Of course every now and then if the weather was hot enough someone could always be seen drenching their head as well. Not recommended, but after sitting in church all morning, often the temptation was too much for some of the older men in attendance. And then sometimes he would be called into one of the stores for candy or a soda and once again a "How's your Daddy Samuel? Anyone interesting staying up on the hill?" would always follow. "No Sir, nobody I know but thank ya for the candy." would be his reply.

As Samuel rounded the corner to the metal truss bridge that spanned over the Ammonoosuc he could see Mary's house up on the hill on South Street. If he stared hard enough he could probably see her in the top window which was her bedroom, or her Daddy sitting on the porch smoking his pipe, but his own Daddy taught him staring was not polite, so he didn't. Instead, he made his way across the bridge, like he did a hundred times before. He passed the feed and grain warehouse where he and his Daddy would pick up supplies, and the train depot across the street from that. The old Beebe house, where his Daddy once told him to stay away from but stopped short at explaining why.

With the afternoon withering on and the early evening preparing itself for the coolness of the night, Samuel walked up the front walk to Mary's front door where he quietly and politely knocked. It only took once before Mary's Daddy came. He stood peering out the screen door at him, not saying anything at first, but studying him up and down. Once he was satisfied or his curiosity was fulfilled enough, deeming him a "decent boy" he hollered up the stairs for Mary.

"Mary! That boy is here and I'm sure I'm not the one he's looking for." he said.

Samuel instantly became embarrassed looking away and shifting from foot to foot.

"Thank you Daddy. I'll be right down." Mary replied in return.

"Thank you Sir." Samuel said low politely.

"Going for a walk this evening? No further than the high school son." Mary's father told him.

He continued as he pulled out his pocket watch. "It takes Mary twenty minutes to walk to school. Fifteen minutes to linger, then twenty minutes back, that should make your return time at exactly eight o'five. Exactly. Not a minute more."

"Yes Sir. Yes Sir. I'll have her back on time Mr. Thompson." replied Samuel with a hint of nervousness in this voice.

Mary's father, a doctor and new to the community, stood before him, holding the screen door ajar with one hand as the other tucked the watch back into his pocket.

"Here I am Daddy. Ohhh Samuel, Daddy isn't making you feel ....well, never mind. We'll be back Daddy." Mary said as she slid past him, grabbing Samuel's hand, skipping down the front steps and walkway.

"I know you will. The boy and I already discussed it." her father called from behind her.

It didn't take long for Mary and Samuel to reach the corner of Main Street at the bottom of the hill. Their excitement of just seeing one another was enough to quicken their pace as well as their giddiness.

"I don't want to go to the school tonight Samuel…" Mary began. Samuel quickly cut her off with nervousness and concern.

"Mary! I told your father…", he began but Mary cut him off too.

"Let's go to the hotel. Just to sit on the front porch. Just for a little while." she said.

"Well. I guess that couldn't hurt, and I'm sure he wouldn't mind. Still, I feel like I'm betraying him a little. I mean, I did say we'd be at the high school." he replied.

"It's not that far away from the school. Besides, he likes your father. And I want to look out over the town. I want to see what you see." she told him.

All Samuel could do was smile at this. "And I bet Ishmae has made ice cream tonight. He said he was going to for the guests who just arrived."

Taking Mary's hand in his, his index finger wrapped around her middle finger. Noticing the unique way he held her hand she commented. "This is neat."

"We are unique. This is our special way we hold hands." Samuel replied to which Mary smiled, squeezing his hand a little tighter.

Samuel retraced his previous walk through town only this time with Mary next to him. Coming across the Union Street bridge, they both looked down to the river and the dam that supplied the power for the grist mill below. That of course led to conversation of one of the first times they met at the bridge. When she told him her name and where she was from. Of how she lived with her father, and that he was a doctor and how her mother had died not so long ago. And he told her of himself, easily, and things he had never talked to anyone before. For a long time he wondered about that and why talking to her was so easy. Telling her how he had never known his mother, that she died not long after he was born, and how he was named after Ishmael, who's full name was Samuel Ishmael, just like his. Of how Ishmael, or Ishmae as mother called him, was like a part of the family and that it was he who first found mother, and father and he calling for the doctor, at her side the entire time. He knew the story. Both his father and Ishmae telling everything about his mother so he would know her as a son should, and not just by a painting or a name. They gave him stories about her. Ones that someday, would be helpful. One's that he could share with his own family.

As they neared the train depot it began raining, lightly. Still holding hands, Samuel steered themselves under the roof on the dock. Glancing inside the window, he could see one man, the telegraph operator, sitting at a desk reading the Courier.

"Next train in isn't for another twenty-five minutes. Let's wait here and watch the rain. We have time." Samuel looked to her.

Mary's smile was indication she liked his idea. "Very romantic Mr. Andersen." was her reply.

"When your with a pretty girl, in the rain, holding hands, what else is there to do?" Samuel chuckled. "Besides. You're my girl, and I…I think…" Beginning so confidently with charm Samuel began fumbling and stumbling with his words, stuttering, not able to finish.

"Samuel? What are you…are you alright?" asked Mary, taking a small step back.

Samuel took a small step back as well. "Mary. You're my girl. And…I love you."

Mary's eyes widened. Then she smiled broadly. "Samuel Andersen. I've been waiting months to hear you say that. And here we are, at a train depot of all places. At least take me out in the rain." Mary giggled to him.

Samuel became a little more at ease at her wit and lightheartedness. "That I can do." Samuel replied, taking her hand again, moving her out from under the rooftop and into the quickening of the falling evening rain.

"Mary. You're my girl. I knew it when I found your ring. And someday, someday Mary, I'm going to not just hand you a ring, but place it on your finger. You're my girl and I love you." stated Samuel with so much confidence and brazen romanticism.

With that they resumed their walk, in their unique way, up over the hill, with a new giddiness and sense of identity of not only themselves but of each other.

19

The Walk

Mary's parents got married on the front steps of her father's house. A two story farmhouse with a broad front porch that carried lazy evenings in rocking chairs passed down three generations. Planted begonias hung in pots across the front, slightly swaying in a night breeze that dried the day's sweat and grit on the backs of necks reddened by an all day sun in the fields. Red clay stained the porch boards and caked boot heels.

They courted for exactly sixteen days. The first week he came every morning with fresh, warm biscuits he made himself, blanketing the red and white picnic blanket on the front lawn. Her father watched out the window, convinced the young man wasn't right in the head. Her mother held her father's hand, not because of the twenty-two years of marriage but to keep his hand off the shotgun standing in the corner. By week two, the picnic breakfasts began fading, replaced with a serenade of a barely playable violin that sounded more like two cats attacking a squirrel. Yet she smiled. The last two days she would descend from her upstairs room, slowly step onto the porch where her beau awaited on bent knee at the front of the steps. Her mother and father watched on, he shaking his head and her smiling, and smiling, nodding and nodding, knowing her daughter had found the one.

Mary and Samuel would walk to an abandoned house at the end of a lonely dirt road once a week. It was a place that reminded Mary of her mother and when the three of them were a family. She, and her mother and father. Holding hands in their special way, index finger entwined around the middle finger, the winding and familiar dirt road, dusty and familiar, wooded or pastured on each side, farms dotting the hills and valley, with the gravel under their feet scrunching stones and pebbles, the only sound. And they were excited, content, happy at simply being together. Where a fall afternoon left the air cool, the weather blue sky perfect, the day to call their own.

And they walked. Until they reached the destination they desired. With the sweet scent of apples in the air. Saying not a word, their gestures, their expressions and holding hands as though for the first time, they stroll together, the orchard calling them in. Rows and rows and rows, branches twisting this way and that, that way and this. Supple and ripe they hung, ready to be plucked, eaten, fulfilled. Behind Mary's house, where her mother too once walked, plucked the ripe fruits from the trees she and her own mother and father had planted, she fell in love with Samuel and became aware that her future was here, with him.

The place, this place, their place. Under a serene blue sky, a single red bird flights from branch to branch, as though saying, "Me. This one. This one." He looked at her when she was not looking. Stealing glances of her moment. She was drawn in with a tantalizing revelation.

Breaking the silence, she whispers, "Do you hear it?"

He nods. "Mmm."

"She is happy we are back. She's been following us since we caught sight of the orchard." replied Mary.

Pink and white petals lay scattered on the ground. Taking her in his arms, the way she loved his arms around her, he bowed his head to the curve of her neck, his lips brushing against her, whispering in return, "The orchard defines you."

He lightly kissed her there. Deliberate. Defined.

Parting, letting her go, knowing what is to come next, he watches her approach a large boulder on the other side of the rows.

Her dress clung to her hips, billowed with each step, a sashay depicting etiquette and poise.

And she places the paper doll, with the many crinkled and faded dolls, onto the rock's rigid surface. Her grace gestures to her steadfast resolve.

Returning back to him he asks, "Another paper doll?"

Mary nods, "Still not enough. I know its a silly thing to do Samuel. But somehow, coming here, Momma and Daddy's favorite place, seeing this big old rock, knowing that Momma would sit here while Daddy would play music for her, I feel closer to her. Cutting out paper dolls and giving them to her, its like we are together again." Mary explained in a weakened voice.

Samuel squeezes her hand a little, in reassurance. "I understand Mary. It's like how I go to Momm's sewing room and run my hand across the fabrics. The same one's she last touched."

Samuel took out a small jackknife then from his pocket, going to the closest apple tree. Turning he asks her, "Mary? Will you stay with me forever?"

She leans against the rock, her hand reaching for the paper dolls scattered there, feeling the paper, withered and yellowed, but still in form, and answers. "Yes. Forever and always."

Turning to the tree, Samuel carves a heart with one word in its center. Trying to peer over his shoulder, Mary leans to see what it is he is carving. She slowly approaches, and he turns, taking her hand, placing it on the carved heart. Feeling the rough bark and the smooth wood from the carving, she looks to him. "Yes?" she asks.

Samuel nods. "The word we will both say on the day we are wedded."

Mary smiles, wrapping her arms around him. They embrace, kiss, their bodies pressed against the other in unbridled romance, as a single paper doll slips from Mary's fingers, fluttering to the ground under the tree, the small red bird lights on the branch near, watches.

20

A Fateful Decision

The night before he was to leave they walked one last time together, their usual route, one step at a time, in a direction they had grown accustomed to.

"I'll be leaving tomorrow.", he told her.

"I know", she said simply, low, almost in whisper.

"Mary, this…", he began, falling short, as though lost to find the words.

She turned him, her eyes studying his face. Slowly, she raised her hand to brush his cheek.

"Don't go Samuel. Change your mind.", she said.

As the park which they stood grew even more quiet from when they entered, the din of the evening rang out with myriad sounds of a world lost in confusion. They were being caught up in a maelstrom and rushed out of control, haphazardly.

"You know I can't do that.", he answered.

Mary, her soft raven hair splaying across her shoulders, framing her face, nodded sadly.

Reaching out to take her hand in his in their special way, Samuel boldly pulled her to him, their bodies but a breath away. He felt her bosom heave at the unexpected and deliberate show of his need for her, his mouth finding her own, an embracing kiss which seemed to embrace the very night. Under the tree, next to the pond, on the path which they had been exploring for months, their desire heightened as their lips moved together like chocolate on silk. Parting the kiss, he whispered against her lips "You're my girl. I'll always be near."

Just then a passing cloud rolled across the harvest moon, briefly blocking out the light.

21

The Carousel

The small town wasn't known for much, other than the half dozen large hotels that catered to the tourists and the occasional passing salesman heading for Canada or perhaps the entertainers from Boston making their way to the big lights and fame of New York City. However, surely the second most thing it was known for, at least to the local area, was the carousel. One of the first wooden structures of Barnum and Bailey Bros. Circus, the carousel was won in a wage,r as rumor had it, some six years back. Something about that or an elephant as the story was told. The carousel was the better choice. And so it is still set in the location where the roustabouts first set it up.

Samuel fingered the dime in his pocket as they neared the ride. He already knew which pony she would choose. They had been coming here all summer, nearly every night, and it didn't take long for him to notice the pattern of her choices. She would choose the blue pony, because the night before it was pink, and the night before that the green one, and before that orange. And so it went, one by one, until she'd come back around to the blue one again. As she stepped aboard, she did just that. Going right for it, he was right behind her, because that's just how it was. And just like that she went into another world, one of dreams and legends, where the hand painted ponies came alive, he was sure of it. All he knew was that he loved her smile and the small giggles she displayed without even realizing it. He could do this all night. Which is why he also only brought one dime with him.

When the carousel slowed, the music fading, he held out his hand to steady her as she stepped off. Holding her briefly about the waist, for that very small moment, was all the magic he needed, knowing that he was there because she wanted him there and that he knew what would happen next. The same thing always happened. An exclamation to the night. His eyes looked to her own as she asked innocently, "What?" and he would only reply "Nothing."

Just then the rain began yet again, the carousel closing down, the attendant covering the gear works, and they hurried themselves to the gazebo. Leftover flyers from the night before littered the floor announcing "Dance the Night to Big Henry's Big Band". Climbing the short steps the rain pelted the rooftop over them, while re-creating the soppy puddles along the marshy lawn. And just like that, as happened each night, they both turned to the other, finding the other's embrace, and their kiss being emboldened by the night rain and the quiet around them.

And they stayed that way, for what seemed like forever. A mutual satisfaction, with only three words needed to make the pack firm and complete.

The climax of their dance arrived with heaving chests and moans of sheer pleasure, no longer soft. Waves of body trembling pleasure gripped them, panting for the end yet secretly wishing for more. And in the end, while they laid next to the other staring up at the stars, their feelings of satisfaction moved through an emotional arc that left them lost but also found and surrendered. They became giddy in their love, talking silly things while being shy and coy. They would name the stars that winked their light down upon them. Sometimes pretending each star named were their children they knew were in their future. Samuel took her hand, holding out her pointer finger to the stars, moving it along, connecting them in a growing portrait.

"These two here. They are called Gemini. The twins. This one here, is Pollux, the brightest, that's you. And this one is Castor. That's me."

"How do you know so much about the stars?" Mary asked, her finger touching the stars that represent themselves.

"Mr. Perry's science class in eleventh grade. I loved the astrology unit." Samuel replied. "It was as though, all these stars had stories of their own you know?"

As they laid there watching the stars, naming and making up stories to fit their themselves, they grew tired, promising the other not to fall asleep, for as the night moved on they knew their family would also be watching the clock, with a growing concern for their whereabouts. So they would rest, play, occasionally dancing a second time before.

They would return back to the gazebo, back to the park, and take the trek through the hillside neighborhoods, back to their homes. She will be starting college soon. And she would be living on her own. For Samuel and she knew their time together was drawing to an end. Every moment, every minute became ever important at an ever quickening pace.

22

The Gazebo Affairs

Meeting each night at the gazebo, just as the light faded away from the day, their youth and restlessness outshone the approaching moonlight. It was as though they couldn't get close enough or spend enough time together or share their thoughts and ideas, dreams, aspirations, or fears. When they held hands it was gentle. When they kissed it was opposite. A fiery passion that built a fever in their bodies that pleaded to be drenched and drowned with a wild abandonment.

They had their meetings timed perfectly. The gazebo was near the small pond, a short walk along a narrow woodland forest adjacent to the park. As the light of the day faded they would arrive at the pond right on time. Dusk grew around them and the canopy of the forest above them darkened their rendezvous, entrusting a tryst they held together in perfect rhythm. The paddy of grass along the pond's embankment was soft and firm, well worn from their prior visits. As they lowered themselves to lie together, their mouths immediately embraced in exploratory kisses of passion. A want. A desire. Pure need as their bodies entwined around the other. Soft moans of pleasure escaped their throats in ecstasy. They needed no words but spoke a language each knew fluently. Their rhyme became one of the lyrics set to their own music. And so they would fall upon the other, night after night, in a greedy lust they called love. Low whispering of the Gemini stars overhead lit their pathway said to them their rhythm and rhyme was not just meant to be but was made to happen long before they knew it. And so they acted. Bodies became one in a dance they alone choreographed and perfected.

As the early evening slowly closed the day's light; as street lamps cast their yellow haloed glow across the streets and sidewalks; as the late night crowd, to which there were few, shadows of themselves cast on brick storefronts made eerie companions, the gazebo affair became distant as they moved forward, ending their night. The rain had just stopped a steady shower since early afternoon, not a drenching kind of rain, but enough to remember the umbrella when going out. Those under the age of twenty, perhaps a little older if lucky enough to feel it, felt the umbrella a waste of time, being more of the fancy free type.

Samuel held her hand in their special way as they walked along, navigating around the small puddles while listening to her talk of her day at the hat shop. Of how Mrs. Dubois, that stingy old spinster from over on Maple Street kept her attention for a full hour and then just walked out of the shop not purchasing anything. That, however, didn't keep his fingers from entwining with her own, a little secret hand hold they held which made their time more memorable. "It's the small things Mary that we'll remember most", he would tell her, and she would reply "You're such an old soul Samuel". Which, he supposed he was.

They had the street almost to themselves, a freight truck or buckboard wagon rattling past them every now and then, wet mud flinging into the air; a couple here and there enjoying the early evening, as much as they were.

"You like working at the hat shop?" Samuel asked, breaking the silence.

"It's alright. Mrs. Dubois is …difficult." she replied, giggling. "But she's nice enough. I have almost what I need saved for the first year of nursing school. Well, for room and board anyway and maybe some books." Mary stated.

"It's coming quickly. Too quickly. Soon, we'll both be in places we've never been before, with folks we never met before, doing things we never done before." Samuel replied, with a hint of nervousness in his voice.

Taking a breath Mary replied in turn. "Ohhh, I know. Sometimes at night, I think about it all before I fall asleep. My chest tightens a little. But then I remember what my Momma use to say when I was just a little girl. 'Mary. Things change. It's as simple as that.' Daddy had a little more to say on the subject a few nights ago when we discussed my moving away." Mary giggled, squeezing Samuel's hand and sashaying her dress in the evening air. As he listened he brushed away a few loose strands of grass.

"He told me change was always happening. 'It's a matter of fact', he said. 'Nothing is permanent, even if you pray for it to be so. He said, 'nature has a way of making us strong and getting us through the difficult times. Just hold on. Just hold on.' And then he pointed up to the sky, even though we were sitting in the parlor…", Mary giggled, continuing, " '…those stars up there know exactly what and where we are going you can be assured. Your mom taught me that when she left this world for her own.' And Samuel, for only the second time ever, I saw his eyes blink back tears." Mary ended with a choked voice.

Samuel pulled her close to him whispering to her, for comfort and for reassurance. "You're my girl Mary and I love you."

Mary laid her head on his shoulder then, whispering in return, for the first time. "I know.   I   love   you   too."

23

Leaving

"This is it," Samuel said.

They both stood on the boarding dock, the train having pulled into the station only moments ago, its steam rolling out from under like a Greek monster ready to swallow up those it carried.

"I hate it that you are leaving. But I want you to. Go. Go right now. Get on that train and I'm just going to walk away.", she replied.

Samuel knew when she was hurting, and knew she protected herself with words she did not mean. Setting down the lone bag which he carried, he reached out for her, pulling her close in a tight embrace. Mary immediately melted into his body, her head against his chest.

"Don't go, Sam. Don't…", she began, but then was awash in sobbing tears that took her voice.

Samuel gently smoothed her back in a tenderness to sooth away her sorrow.

"Shhhh. I know. I know….the quicker I leave, the quicker I come home.", he said.

Mary, catching her breath, Sam's embrace seeming to take effect in calming, returned, "Come back to me. Please."

"I will.", was all he could say. And then, "You're my girl."

They kissed a longing and lingering kiss that pushed past the flirtatiousness of their relationship, still in its early stages at only six months. People came and went, paying very little attention, just two more people being separated by a war seven thousand miles away. Sounds of the train as it released its steam only to mount it back, by the shovel full, of coal at the head of the long line of passenger cars. Somewhere near a small child cries and the conductor announces time to board.

Samuel ran his finger over Mary's cheek, wiping away the tears that settled there. "I'll be alright you know. I'll write every chance I can. Take care of your father and help him with his patients. Help at the hotel with my father. Send me some of Ishmae's bread and jam.", he told her as he separated from her a little more.

"I will", Mary replied back. "I will.", and she smiled then, with a small laugh.

"That's my girl. Smiling still.", Samuel said.

"Wait a minute. Hold on. I need a photograph." came the voice of his father.

Standing there, as though coming out of thin air, was his father, holding a camera.

"One photograph. For a memorable occasion. Mary, stand next to my son."

And they did. Posing for the camera, for Samuel's father, for others who watched and moved around them. And like hundreds of thousands of other young men, Samuel turned then, picking up the one bag which he packed and half turned, looking toward the open door of the train. Then, turning back to her, Samuel leaned softly to her, as he whispered to her ear his affection.

'I love you. You're my girl.", he whispered, kissing the lobe of her ear. Mary replied back in her own response, "I know. I love you too."

Turning again, he walked to the open train door, stepping inside.

Mary placed her fingers to her ear, where she felt his lips only moments ago, while watching him inside the car, jostling around others, finding his seat. Sliding down the window, he stuck out his hand and Mary hurried over to grasp it.

Connected once again, they both said the same inaudible words.

"I love you." as their mouths formed the words that carried them both away from the other and into a very real and uncertain time.

The train pulled away, their hands lost grip, Mary left standing and staring as the train picked up steam, pulling further and further down the track.

"I'll be here.", she mumbled with a trembling and uncertain voice.

24

Overseas

Samuel had been in Germany for three weeks for basic training. He then did two more weeks behind the front lines, and then five days in the trenches. In less than six weeks Samuel found himself lying in a makeshift field hospital for two weeks before it was safe to transport the wounded further behind the lines. Between mortar rounds and the constant barrage of machine gun fire across the trenches, any kind of movement was nearly impossible. Only two trenches were safe enough to move about. The one where Samuel laid now, and the one perpendicular running north. The Germans were dug in deep, and well planned, prepared for many days of fighting. In that time, he learned he was the only member of his unit who came out of the battle alive. Sixty-four men are gone. Except for him. He also learned from one of the corp men; he was found wandering, clothes torn and mostly blown off his body, from trench to trench calling out names that were not part of his unit, nor names any of the corp men had ever heard of before. Mr. Sylvester, Mrs. Dubois, Miss EmmaLee Jean Harold, and Samuel Masterson. Names he would mutter to himself for the next few days as he lay fighting to regain his senses.

Left paralyzed and shell shocked from the mustard gas and mortar, he could neither talk, walk, or make use of his arms and hands. At times his sight became so blurred nothing around him was familiar, but strange objects of colored hues, blended in a mess and scrambled. His hearing was often tinny, at random times. And when he did regain some movement he would often cover his ears all day in a feeble effort to block out all sound. Lost in a world he no longer recognized, he found himself praying to die. The pain would go away and he would no longer need to listen to those around him in more dire straits than he. Surrounded by the dying as you yourself lie dying is like succumbing to a nightmare wrought on by nightmares you had as a child. But one image, not of a nightmare, but of experiences he will always cherish, met his days and nights with an air of zest and zeal. Mary. Her smile. Standing at the carousel, just stepping off; her arms out; he caught her on his own. The two of them. Giddy, and happy together. But Mary was always in his thoughts. It was her standing on the front porch of the hotel. Mary at the gazebo. Mary is sitting cozily near the pond. A picnic. Mary's hand in his own. The way they would walk. Holding hands. And they would entwine their fingers, in that special way. A low word, 'walk?' A light nod. Communication is no longer needed. Both knowing the other, such as the connection they shared. I t was those images he held on to. It was those images, of Mary, that would keep him alive, and bring him back home.

He left the field hospital and the trenches that reeked of mustard gas, blood, and death, and the bodies of his friends. His vision returned, no longer blurring. His hearing was no longer tinny, though he still covered his ears whenever a plane was low and overhead. What did stil linger, was the paralysis in his hands. He couldn't squeeze or clench them with any degree of strength. Even the slightest would make him wince in pain. The doctors told him they would never properly heal, recover to where he could clench a fist. If he was a boxer, his career was over.

"Samuel? Is there a Samuel here? No last name?", cried out a hospital orderly.
Samuel had been standing by the floor to ceiling windows of the old catholic church, looking out over the fields in the direction where he came close to dying and where his entire unit had been killed.
"Yes. Yes, yes. That's me.", he exclaimed back as he turned from the window to face the voice.
A young man, no older than high school age, came toward him, a clipboard and chart in hand, as he scanned the written copy, his eyes barely averting to meet him.
"Says here you are to be on-board the HMS'' Hilary at 010:00 hours.", said the orderly, only briefly surveying Samuel to see if he was actually listening.
"Oh? On-board? As in….leaving?"Samuel replied in shocked curiosity.
"If you don't want to leave just say so, there are a hundred others right behind you.", said the orderly.
"What? Ohhh, no. No. Of course not. I mean, of course I want to leave. What time…? Ohhhh shit. That's in ten minutes!", said Samuel enthusiastically.
The orderly returned simply, "I suggest you get packed." moving on to the next set of beds and patients.
And he did. Reaching under his bed where he kept a small bag of clothes, he tucked it under his arm running toward the front double doors.

"Have you heard from Samuel Mary?", asked Mary's father, as he stood just behind her in the side garden.
"Hmmm? Oh no Daddy. Sorry. No. Not today.", Mary replied.
"Ahhh. Well. Perhaps tomorrow then." said her father.
Mary continued to read the letter, from her cousin Betsy over in Carroll County. Or, at least she pretended to read. She really didn't. How could she read anything when Samuel's

letter was over two months old? Hurriedly, she ran inside, up the back staircase, to her bedroom. Going to her vanity dresser, she reached for the letter, the last letter, she had tucked in a corner on the mirror. Carefully removing the letter from the envelope, something she did like a ritual each night before going to bed, she unfolded it again and began reading.

23, Feb. 1917

Dear Mary,

It is me, Samuel. Just a few quick words to say I am fine. We are in a country I can not pronounce. Something 'burg or something or other. Anyway, we are marching to the front lines in the morning, some hundred fifty miles away. Don't worry now. I know what you are thinking as you read this. But I'll be fine. I know it. As long as I can still see your smile, I know it to be so. Rumor is that this might be our last mission together. Seems the army is in need of more young and lively young men. I go to go Mary. Final inspection before the morning. I love you Mary. You're my girl.

Yours,

Sam

She read it again before gently taking care of the letter, sliding it and it's envelope back into the edging of the mirror. Looking at herself, she whispered, "Come back to me Samuel. Come back to me. Please."

"What do you mean delayed? How can an entire steamliner be delayed? The Atlantic waters are safe now.", cried Samuel to the clerk in the booth. With graying hair and a hunched back, the man looked to be in his early eighties. In fact, Sam had begun to notice that it is more common now. The majority of folks were either the elderly and infirmed or the young kids not old enough to be of service to the military yet. Anyone between the ages of eighteen and forty five was quite difficult to find.

"I'm really very sorry Sir. It's quite out of our hands. Now, would you be interested in some soup? I'm always willing to share my wife's cooking.", replied the clerk.

Samuel looked around, up and down the dock, out over the horizon.

"Delayed. Wonderful.", was all Samuel could muster in reply.

At the mention of 'home' Samuel felt both sad and confused. He knew the word. Knew its definition. Could give examples of what home meant and is. But what he couldn't do is place himself inside the word. That is, it seemed he had no real experience to relate himself to such a place.

The reverberations of the crashing waves against the pier below hypnotized him for hours. What began in the early morning of him rushing to secure his passage, ended with him in the same place, the day closing. High tide was making its mark on the surrounding beaches, people diminished quickly to what was a busy place of incoming and outgoing folks, departing one ship while others boarded another. Now it was only he who stood on the pier, transfixed and memorized on a horizon to which he became lost.

A faint chime broke the hold. A church bell in the distance. Ringing in the evening; giving reminders for mass. Running a hand through his hair, he quickly glanced around, his chest gasping, heaving for air as though an invisible weight had been lifted and he was rescued from a drowning pool. Pulling his other hand from his pant pocket, he looked to two, half melted and folded metal discs reading the name. "Samuel A." it read. "5'8" 165 lbs. Eyes Blue Hair Brown BT AB" Rubbing each together between his fingers and thumb, he had no notion of what to make of them. Instead, he followed the chime of the bell. Finding the cobbled stone street, he meandered in and out of lanes and alleys until he stood in front of a towering stone and wooden church, the bell tower the culprit that drew him in. A man and woman walked past him as he stood opposite the street, watching as they ascended the steps to the great wooden doors, a priest standing silently in welcome. As the couple entered another approached doing the same, then a lone elderly man, a mother and daughter, holding hands, the little girl, perhaps only six, holding tight onto a doll. He became caught up in the pattern, in the routine of those who took each step, entering the church, becoming lost to him to whatever awaited them. Curiosity grew inside of him. He too took a step, then another, and upon taking the third, he caught the image of himself in a store front window. He stopped immediately. Turning to face the reflection, he saw himself standing there. Dressed in a military uniform, high brown boots, green trousers and jacket. The one stripe on his shoulder indicating private and infantry. Reaching back into his pocket, he again pulled out one of the two metal discs. "Samuel A.", he whispered to himself. Suddenly, turning away and rounding the corner, not even glancing back to the church, he knew exactly where he must go.

Samuel returned back to his unit's base just before the end of day inspection. Entering the barracks his best friend, together since the day they shipped out of Norfolk, Virginia five years ago, immediately caught his appearance.

"Andersen, where have you…", he began but stopped short. "My God, what happened to you? Where have you been?"

"I uh, this morning…", Samuel began, looking around, still a bit confused as to just how his day did transpire. "I was at the hospital. Getting checked out for these headaches I've been having. And my hands of course.", he said, squeezing and massaging each hand as he answered. "I got word I was to be shipped home…I mean out early this morning. To report to dockside onboard a steamer. Only it was delayed. Delayed."

"What?", his friend asked curiously. "There are no steamers or any other kind of ship transporting anyone back home buddy. Any ship, small boat, fishing trawler or any other kind of floating vessel have all been commissioned for relief efforts. Samuel, we were told that last week.", his friend laid a hand on his shoulder. "You alright pal? What's happened to you?"

Samuel stood there, dumbfounded, feeling the butterflies of nervousness once again enter the pit of his stomach.

"You've been gone all day Sam. Have you been to the docks?", his friend asked, taking a faint smell of his uniform. "The salt air is fresh."

"No. No. At a church actually. Only I never went in. For evening mass. I watched others." Samuel replied.

"That's it. You're coming with me. Back to the hospital. Right now.", said his friend.

Taking Sam's arm, he walked willingly out of the barracks. "Hey. Randolph? Let the Sarge know I"ve taken Andersen here to the hospital. Medical emergency. It couldn't wait.", his friend shouted at another.

"Your hands are weak, but that's to be expected. Nothing unusual since the last time I checked. I'm sure it's the headaches you are having. Daytime hallucinations paired with a blackout. That's what happened to you. I"ve seen it before. Your mind is making up a story to how you want to see all of this end. It's stressful. Fatigue. Very typical for soldiers at war.", the doctor stated.

"I blanked an entire day doc. An entire day. I'm a little scared about that.", Samuel replied.

"Keep taking the headache powders. One packet in the morning, another if you need it. No more than two a day.", said the doctor.

Samuel nodded sliding off from the gurney. "Alright.", was all he could say.

Walking back out into the brightness of the day, he shaded his eyes from the light, squinting as he eyed his friend.

"I'll live.", Sam said.

"Ah huh. Until you don't. I'm watching you. Seriously. I want to know how you are feeling every morning you get up and each night before you close those stupid eyes.", his friend replied back.

'Yeah, yeah. Let's get out of here. ``I'm sure the Sergeant is worried sick about me too.'', said Sam.

"So bad, he'll give you double the workload.", his friend said with a chuckle.

"Congratulations Mary. This is a proud, proud day. No one has studied and worked as hard as you.", said Mary's father. Dr. Thompson was indeed proud of his daughter. Since she was old enough to walk, he had been bringing her with him to his house calls. While he met with patients, his daughter, a delight to everyone, so well mannered, would either watch from across the room, her father, not just administering medicines but providing the understanding and gentle demeanor his patients needed for their afflictions. Not even the families who had children her age, did she really want to play with. Watching her father at work was far too important to miss then playing with paper dolls or looking at the comics. When she announced at only age fourteen she was going to be a nurse, it was of no real surprise to her mother, especially not to her father.

"Thank you father. You are my inspiration.", she replied, kissing him affectionately on his cheek.

"You know, now that the war is over, Samuel should be coming home soon. Any word from him by chance?", her father asked.

"Not a word. And I'm so worried. I haven't even received a single letter for eight months now. I was getting one a week for the first two years. Then he was brought to the front lines, so well, not getting any then was to be expected. But since he was wounded, they were starting again with consistency.", she said.

"Hmmm. I'm going to write to Senator Davies. See what he can find out. He owes me a favor since the birth of his grandson last year. That, and …other unmentionables.", her father said the former aloud, the latter as a mutter.

Mary smiled, nodded, dipping her chin, a sudden melancholy coming over her. The front parlor room of their home held a dozen or more townsfolks, all friends and medical professionals her father often held an audience with, all paying tribute to her on graduation day. Walking across the room to the punch bowl, she poured another glass of the orange jubilee, turning to watch the coming and going and listening to the polite conversations about the room. Nodding with social grace, smiling here, silent affirmations for those present, gesturing her thank yous as she was taught at an early age when her mother would drag her from one social event to another. Glancing out the window, she noticed her best friend Chloe cross the porch to the front door. She and Chloe had been friends since they both could walk, Chloe often coming along for all day outings with her and her mother. Being in the same class all through primary school and later high school, she and Chloe became known as sisters, not just best friends.

"Chloe. Chloe. Over here.", Mary waved.

"Mary.", replied Chloe, crossing the room with a ladylike demure. Chloe often caught the eye of every young man who happened to be in the same room as her, and today was no exception. It seemed the entire room became silent, to a standstill, as Chloe Roberts sashayed her way to her friend.

"Oh Mary. This is lovely. You so deserve it darling.", Chloe commented. "And look at you, you are ravishing. Wait...wait, what is this?", she commented, glancing into her friend's eyes. "Tears? Of joy I hope."

"Oh they are. But, well, father asked about Samuel, so, well, I did get a little weepy I guess. But I'm fine now.", Mary answered.

"Mary. It's been over a year since Samuel went to Europe. And what, at least two since you last heard from him. I mean, I'm sure he's fine and all, but sometimes...oh Mary. I do hope he comes home to you. But, but what if he doesn't?", Chloe asked, never having been one to mince words.

"I have thought of it. And I have been thinking of taking a trip overseas. As a nurse I can be useful while also looking for Sam. Especially in Paris, where I last heard from him.", said Mary in a serious tone.

Bringing her aside to talk low, Chloe replied, "Does your father know of this plan of yours?"

"Well. No. Not exactly. And he's not going to either. Is he?", replied Mary sternly.

"Not an utterance from my mouth sister, promise. But expect a lecture when you do tell him.", replied Chloe.

"Who says I will.", returned Mary.

"Mary Thompson. You scoundrel.", laughed Chloe, as the two of them giggled like they have always done.

A week later after his incident, Samuel laid on his cot, half asleep from the morning work detail and half awake in anticipation for the afternoon inspection. Being one of only a handful at the barracks, it was quiet and soon he found himself in a dream-like world. He was seated on a bench at a gazebo, just he, alone, while overhead the zinging of mortars and the green flashes of flares brightened the sky. As he looked around, a carousel came into view, only instead of brightly painted horses, they were blacked with the grime and grit of a battlefield. A shadow appeared from behind one of the horses. Then he watched himself, dressed as a young man just out of high school, offering his hand to a beautiful young girl. It seemed, in his dream, he would know her name, but couldn't place it.

He awoke with a startled moan, sitting upright, sweating profusely. The room was completely empty now, the few others who he shared quarters with gone. Looking around the room, he had no idea where he was. He recognized nothing. Not the neatly made cots; foot lockers; nothing. Dressed in a white Tshirt and his detail pants, he swung his legs out from under the blankets, pulling on the boots that were there. In a nervous and frightening moment, peering out the small windows that lined each side of the barracks, he hastened himself across the room to the back door, opening it slowly, quietly. Glancing out, seeing no one, Samuel Andersen, as he was known less than two years before, disappeared.

Mary placed the last of her garments in the steamer trunk she was taking with her. Downstairs she could still hear her fathers boisterous sentiments on the reasons why her departure from the town in which she grew up, and the practice which he would soon hand to her, was nothing more than folly and foolish. But she knew what she needed to do. She felt it from some deep down inside place that going to Paris was the right thing. She told her father, her friends, and even sometimes herself that it was to put her nursing skills to work to help heal the wounds of the locals across the French countryside. Only Chloe knew the real reason why she was saying goodbye. To search for Samuel.

"It's not a goodbye when you take up an effort to find someone you love.", she had said earlier. Her father listened. Had nothing to say to that. For not so long ago, he had said the very same when her mother became sick. An ailment that affected her brain and her sense of who she was. Her father guessed a tumor of some kind, and he wasn't wrong. Throughout her disease she became a little more confused, a little more incoherent, and a lot more lost. Her father began reading to her aloud. Favorite books they both once enjoyed. He told her he was searching for her. Through the words they once shared. "I'm not ready to say goodbye to her yet. I'm going to find her again before she leaves. Just one last time.", he explained to her.

So Mary was taught that and she learned to take that chance when you felt it was the right thing to do. "This is the right thing to do.", she said aloud to herself as she closed the trunk lid, securing the leather strapping.

Descending the staircase, she found her father at the bottom, quiet now, a solemn look on his face. "I suppose this is it then.", he said to her.

"It is. It's not goodbye father. I will return. With Samuel.", she replied back.

Her father nodded understandingly. "I know." Leaning to her, he gave a calming and quiet kiss to her brow, wrapping his arms around his daughter one final time before she walked out her family's front door. As she did so, he called her name. "Mary."

She turned to look at her father. "I would do the same. I'm proud of you.", he said.

Mary smiled at him as only a daughter can do with her father. "I love you papa.", she told him, then turned, walking down the walkway where the car awaited.

Samuel unloaded the crates off the cart, stacking them on the sidewalk where a boy took them inside the small market.

"Sam. Hurry now Sam. The sun has risen and the people need their vegetables.", the seventy year old French shopkeeper said while standing at the door.

Sam's French was not good but he was learning. Handing the last crate to the boy he wiped his hands on the apron he wore about his waist. "Here JP. Last one.", he said.

Jean-Pierre was the boy's name, JP the shortened version Sam used for him. It made him feel rather important and a little more grown up when Sam called him by it.

25

Letters

Dear Mary,

I wish you could be here. Paris is a city of lights, just as it's written. Of course I don't see too much being here on the army base. They have us stationed and closed up pretty good every day with little time for anything fun like seeing the city. We did all get a furlough a few days ago for twenty four hours. Of course that was if you were able to use it after three days of nothing but running, climbing, fighting each other in hand to hand matches, and all the calisthenics they love watching us do. I did get out nevertheless, for a few hours. Went to a little cafe where I had what's called a croissant. Basically a piece of light and fluffy bread with butter. It was good, but not as good as back home. Let my mom know that, it will make her smile.

Mary. I miss you. I've been thinking a lot about us lately. The carousel. Our meeting place at the gazebo. The walk to our pond where nobody can find us. Just sitting on the porch at my parents' hotel watching the lights of the town. Your dress. The yellow one. I'd be a liar if I said no to that. Holding your hand. Your laugh. But perhaps most of all your smile. The way you tilt your head just so; your little laugh as your eyes smile. The place behind your ear that I kiss that brings that smile out a little wider.

Promise me something Mary. This war, it's going to be a long one. We aren't going to be home by Christmas as everyone was telling us. The Germans are dug in deep, and they mean business. Half of France is devastated in ruin as is everywhere the Germans have marched. Promise me Mary, that if I do not make it back, you will go on. Live. Because you deserve to be kissed. Everyday. By a man who knows the words as well as the way he shows you. Live passionately. With intent. No regrets.

And if I do return home Mary, I promise you all those things. Everyday. I will kiss you in the morning, because you are beautiful in the morning. I will hold your hand on long walks; my arms will wrap you up in comfort when you need it most. Because we all need to feel that kind of embrace. I will love you with desire. With every breath.

I wrote this the other night for you. I do a lot of writing while laying in my bunk. It's hard to sleep sometimes. Imagine a room of sixty other guys. Snoring and restless and constantly getting up to use the latrine. My bunk is just below a small porthole window so I get a little bit of light from the outside lamppost. Anyway, this is what I came up with. I hope you like it.

In a breath of a moment I became lost...
   "i touched her lips, she smiled;
   her eyes glowed, shone with a million twinkling stars.
   their illumination guiding me to the heaven of soft, translucent light, for the Desire we both ached, yearned, seeked.

In a breath of a moment...
   i touched her hair;
   the smell of each strand leaving me captivated,
   leaving me stunned, hungry for more.

i caressed her neck, curves of her shoulders, her chest;
   and she caught breath, small silent moans
   And i heard-
   heard and listened, capturing her sound with the desire of my own mouth.

trembling, parted lips, her eyes delicately closed, hair hung loose as my
   fingers entwined-
   her mouth hungry for mine-
   as free in our ecstasy, i gave back to her, to her cry...

In a breath of a moment...
   To her cry, no longer a sigh.

And I do Mary. I have been praying a lot lately. I am sure that would make my mother happy. She always wanted me to go to church more. Sometimes it takes twelve thousand miles and a whole lot of homesickness and heartache to realize that what you have right in front of you is worth everything. You are right in front of me Mary. I pray I will come back to you.
   I love you Mary. You're my girl.
   Your Samuel.

Dear Mary,

Remember the night we played cribbage? And you so enjoyed winning. Your laughter. That's what I hear now. Your laugh. And it gets me through. I just think of your laugh, and suddenly the push-ups, the sit-ups, and all the jumping jacks sergeant screams at us to do, they no longer matter. I just do them.

I got your letter Mary. The mail is really slow over here. It was written four weeks ago. It is good you are helping your father at the office. All that waiting on patients will help to get into nursing school. That and a little of your father's influence of course.

When I leave Mary, I mean discharged and leave Europe, and come back home, father wants me to take over the hotel. I suppose I could. I mean, I suppose I should. It is what father has been expecting. I am going to need help though. I am hoping you might want to do it too. After nursing school of course. I know that is important to you.

Mary, I need to go. The sergeant is yelling.

I love you. You're my girl.

Your Samuel.

Mary folded the three letters placing each carefully back inside the envelopes they were delivered in. Only three letters. He had only written three and then they just stopped.

26

A Night Out

Working at the market became a respite long needed after months in the hospital. The confines of medicine paired with physically ill patients, most of whom were left maimed and limbless, was daunting and filled with dis-spirit. Being around such, a few of the boys he became good friends with over the last two months, began taking its toll on his own emotions. The Second Battle of the Somme, for the thirteen days it lasted, became Samuel's talisman. It represented the only memory he had. Everything before, where he lived, how he grew up, who his parents were, if he was married or had a girlfriend or not, all was gone. He had no knowledge of who he was prior to that front line. The two small circular, metal disks in his pocket were the only things he had of who he was. Samuel A. Blood Type AB. Religion Catholic. Birthday May 10, 1896. Thumbing the only identity he had in his pocket, he gazed out the window in anxious anticipation, an elation that gave some hope of leaving the hospital, if only for a few hours, to work at the market and the family who so generously accepted him.

There was Monique. Daughter of Etienne Durand, the shopkeeper of the tiny market on Rue Cler where he worked, keeping the front walk swept, the vegetable bins filled, carrying crates of wine from the vineyard wagons, and trying hard not to see her. An impossible task. Slight frame with raven straight hair, lips full in both smile and in astute appearance when speaking; eyes dark, often gleaming with excitement and surprise of secrets kept close. He noticed her. He could not help himself. Her father was also slim of build. Nearing his fiftieth year, Monsieur Etienne Durand was a proud Parisian of humble means. Operating the market each morning gave him the purpose and meaning of who he was as a Frenchman. Having never once closed the small store throughout the war, gave him much pride, not for himself, but for his country. The perseverance of a Frenchman to never surrender was indeed present to his very core character.

"Samuel. You are cleared to take leave for the afternoon if you wish.", said the doctor on duty that day.

Turning, Samuel faced the voice, an older man who he had gained a mutual friendship with over the weeks.

"Perfect. Thanks Doc. I have a job to get to you know.", replied Samuel.

Chuckling a bit, "Just don't over do it. Remember, physically you are fine. But in your head the war is not over. If you find yourself lost, not knowing where you are or who you are, remember in your pocket is my name and the address of the hospital. Show it to someone. That shopkeeper Monsieur Durand. He knows what to do. I've spoken to him.", returned the Doctor.

"Got it right here.", said Samuel, as he pulled out a folded piece of paper with the hospital address on it.

"Then off with you. Your day awaits.", said the doctor then adding, "And so does Monsieur Durand's daughter."

Samuel looked to him in surprise, a bewildering shock as though a silent proclamation that he surely did not know what he was speaking of. The doctor merely laughed, turned, exited the room to visit the next.

At the market, Samuel tied the apron he wore around his waist, immediately tending to the jobs about the store. With the war coming to an end more and more items were coming in. As a local market place, the store relied on locals to keep the shelves stocked. From fresh vegetables to fresh fruits, to breads and cheeses, wine and beer, and now, as he gently and delicately placed each baked good under the glass countertop, chocolates and pies and cakes and croissants and eclairs. Business was picking up, with the vast array of Europeans coming and going to and from the city, country to country, as far away as America. Americans themselves could now be seen on almost every Parisian street, staying late hours, particularly with the young french girls. Samuel wasn't immune t0 such carefree and buffaroonary. Still being a patient, he had his limits of course. And still suffering from the migraines and the occasional blackouts kept him from being discharged as a fulltime patient and especially with the Army as an enlisted soldier. But his eyes certainly did meet Moniques. She quickly became his 'breath of fresh air' as he likened her to be, to himself. Sorting apples into outside bins or waiting on a customer, Samuel never missed a chance to take her in. The way she moved. A deliberateness and intention. Not an ounce of energy wasted did she perform her duties around the store; nor the way she spoke. With few words for ordinary conversation, but if on a passionate topic her intellect and knowledge of such was noteworthy and impressive. His appeal to her was not in a physical way, but it was undeniable to him, as he was very much aware, yet, he panged to be close to her This feeling seemed to be familiar territory but he had no idea why. Was he married? Was there a girlfriend waiting for him to return home? If so, he could not fathom the memory of such. So he concentrated on what he knew, on what he felt presently. It was though he already knew her. That instead of having only met her and her father only weeks before, it seemed like he had known her all his life. Her mannerisms. The tilt of her head. The smile in her eyes. The common phrases she used in speech. When she said 'oi' it made him smile and chuckle a bit. Despite not knowing one another, she made him feel comfortable. The small flirtations they tossed at one another confirmed his feelings for her. They had a connection, deep and powerful, that drew them together. And he was interested.

"Papa, I will be home late this evening. There's a show at Le Trianon. A real live show Papa!", declared Monique to her father.

"Who will you be with?, " stated Etienne as matter-of-factly as only a father can to his daughter.

"Oh Papa. Just Jeanne and Bernadette. From school. You remember? A real live show Papa. It's been so long.", swooned his daughter with obvious excitement.

"I'll keep the store lights on. And I'll be waiting up. You will not be out past midnight.", said her father, the last words ending the conversation.

Kissing her father tenderly on the cheek, Monique ran up stairs to her bedroom. From the corner of the store Samuel watched the exchange. A show at a theater? Has he ever been to such a place? The thought of finding out was tempting. Approaching Ettiene he asked, "Where is this theater?"

Turning to him, looking up from the register book which he had returned his concentration on, he replied, "Eighty Boulevard de Rochechouart, near Montmartre. You aren't thinking of going are you?",asked Ettienne, looking at him, measuring his well being.

"I don't know. What kind of place is it?" Samuel asked.

"It's a musical theater. A concert hall. Where you listen.", said Etienne, tugging at his ear with a smirk, then adding, "while flirting with the young ladies in their new dresses."

"Oh." was all Samuel could say, perhaps a little embarrassed.

"You should go un Jeune Homme," said Etienne. "Chaperone my daughter. I would feel more comfortable if someone I knew and trusted was with her."

Samuel's heart actually skipped a beat at hearing this. Untying his apron, he folded it and handed it to him. "Well. I shouldn't be late then.", he said with a laugh. "Will you send word to the hospital and my doctor to let him know where I will be? He will not take kindly to my decision, but I feel compelled and I can not be a patient forever. It's been too long as it is. Assure him I will be careful. I know what to do."

Placing his hand on Samuel's shoulder the kindly old man nodded, "I will take care of it. You do this for me. Wait here. I have a suit for you. My sons. May he rest in Heaven above."

Etienne hurriedly went to the back of the store, where he soon reappeared with a draped suit, complete with pants, vest, shoes, and french style cufflink shirt.

"It will fit. You and my son are the same size.", said Ettienne with a tremble in his voice.

Samuel took the offering, holding it up, as though cherishing the meaning and recognizing the importance of the moment for the old man. He looked to Ettienne, nodding in assurance he would wear it proudly and preserve his son's name and integrity in a public audience.

Situated in the garden of the Elysee Montmartre, the cafe Trianon was first designed and began construction only two years before Samuel's birth. The following year it became one of Paris' first music halls. With ample floor space to seat two hundred and with its double balconies rising to its domed ceiling, Le Trianon quickly gained fame for its musical production, with Jeanne -Marie Bourgeois becoming known for not only her voice but her comedic roles as well, while later gaining even more attention with her shapely legs in the more risque routines, which found her eventually at the infamous Moulin Rouge. With red satin backed theater seating and the walls painted gold, highlighted with Greco-Roman style frieze along the balcony, cornices, and moldings, the theater was both opulent and luxurious in style and flair. As he approached, with both of Monique's friends on each arm, and she linked arm in arm with friend at her left, the short walk to the theater on a warm, early evening was a stroll that was nourishing for his very soul. He found himself comfortable with both her friends, they being accepting of his gentlemanship, conversing with him almost the entire way. It was almost as though he had lived here in Paris all of his life. He could certainly get used to the lifestyle and the friendliness of the people.

As the four of them walked through the garden, the abundance of beauty was all around. Roses of red, yellow, pink, and orange abounded in their blooms, while irises and dahlias aligned in rows alongside azaleas and rhododendron. Walkways in and out of these fragrant blooms created a picturesque and romantic feel. Vendors with carts of cut flowers as well as chocolatiers offered their wares to the couples along the way. Yet, for Samuel, he realized he had no associations with any other garden or city before this one. He knew the flowers, could name them, but could recollect no actual experience. He knew what chocolate tasted like. A sullenness came over him, one which Monique noticed but did not show her concern. Instead, it was Bernadette who spoke up.

"Monsieur Samuel, what is the trouble? Your pallor has grown pale?", she asked.

Samuel slowed his step, tilting his head to her, "Has it?" he replied.

"I do hope we are of good company.", Bernadette added.

"Perhaps you and Monique should change places, Bernadette. Maybe its Monique's arm he sullens for.", giggled Jeannette mischievously.

Monique's embarrassment was plain. "I am privileged to have each of your arms this night my dear.", said Samuel as he patted Jeannette's and Bernadette's hands.

Samuel became self conscious as they stood in line for the theater. His experience with Parisian crowds came from either the hospital or the streets along the way to the market. Not many patients at the hospital were able to move around, the majority being invalids, while he always took the least crowded streets. Dressed in the latest Paris fashions, language flourished all around him. He knew enough French since his stay to pick up the gist of meaning, while there were also English speaking people there as well. A few military officers dressed in their fancy bearing their rank and ribbons. He suddenly felt conscious about not wearing his own uniform. Yet, he had no uniform to wear, his own went to the burn pile a long time ago to prevent disease. So as they slowly stepped their way inside the lobby, showing their tickets to the usher, Samuel began memorizing everything about the theater, the people, the garden and walk, and even more so of Monique. He had only seen her dressed in her working attire: plain dress with pockets, apron, sometimes a scarf, and black heeled shoes. Tonight was different. Suddenly Jeannette and Bernadette began whispering rather loudly, pointing, rather obviously, over to their right. Glancing to what captured their attention so he could decipher nothing of interest himself, but the two girls sure could, pulling themselves from his arm, sidling over to their new interest.

Shortly, only Samuel and Monique were left standing together.

"Well, it seems I have been abandoned.", Samuel stated.

"Seems so.", replied Monique shyly.

Looking around a bit, trying to avoid eye contact but not wanting to at the same time, Samuel broke the silence.

"I did promise your father I'd look out for you.", said Samuel as he offered his arm.

"Did you? He made you promise, didn't he?", she replied.

"He may have suggested. But I made the promise freely.", said Samuel.

Monique smiled at this.

As they moved closer to the front, each handing over their ticket, they glanced around for their friends but could not see them.

"They are grown. I'm not worrying about them. As long as they stay together they will be fine.", said Monique.

"Then tonight belongs to you and I. Shall we?", said Samuel, as he escorted her into the theater.

"My handsome soldier. Lead me.", she said back.

Dressed in a strapped gown of blue satin, Monique carried herself with grace, finesse, and a sophistication befitting French Royalty. Her movements were fluid and intentional, the same she conducted at her father's market. He found himself more intrigued with her than with the theater itself.

Finding their seats in the balcony, they moved together silently, neither quite knowing what else to say to the other. Yet, in that silence, a comfort of not needing to say anything for the sake of making conversation. It seemed to be of a natural and mutual understanding. A connection between them written in gesture and manner. As they seated themselves, Samuel reached for her hand, holding hers gently and inviting. He liked the way her hand fitted in his own. The way their fingers entwined and as the house lights dimmed, leaving the theater in darkness, they brushed their fingers together in a secret flirtation only they knew.

27

A New Feeling

That evening was something Sam was not expecting. Something. The only word he could accurately define it as. What had begun as a curiosity and inquiry with Monique's father, turned into he becoming her father's eyes and daughter's protector. Somewhere inside of him he was not only honored to do so, but also realized he was her escort to a theatrical performance in a Paris evening, with friends and hundreds of Parisians who would undoubtedly be watching them. Together. As a couple who were obviously enjoying one another's company. Somewhere inside of him he liked that thought. He liked the city. He liked his job. And though he was still enlisted in the U.S. Army and a patient at the hospital, he was also near to being discharged on both accounts. His amnesia seemed to be permanent with no progress of recovering any former memories of who he was before Paris. But that didn't bother him. He liked this new life. And the night of the theatre he realized he liked Monique. He enjoyed being with her. He liked her closeness. He liked her smile. And, he imagined, he would come to like the feel of her hand in his. Last night he held her hand for the first time. She did not mind. With fingers laced together, it felt as natural as did the silence to which they sat. There was no certainty of who he was before. What his life was like. There was only the reality that he was living in now. And that feeling was important to him. Monique became his breath of fresh air.

"Thanks for coming last night Samuel.", Monique told him as they both unloaded vegetable crates from the wagon.

Samuel hesitated. Since arriving at the market, he had no idea what to say or how to act around her. Last night left him stunned and stuttering in his thoughts.

After some time that seemed like an eternity he managed to spit out a response.

"My pleasure. It was a lovely evening. I was happy to comfort your father.", he replied.

Monique dropped her head, stood still for a moment, in obvious disappointment.

Samuel picked up on her demeanor right away. Was he always this foolish around women? Or just Monique who he was beginning to feel deeply?

Setting down a crate he held on the buckboard, he recovered.

"That is. Miss Monique, I had a wonderful time and would not have wanted to be with anyone other than the Mademoiselle standing before me."

Monique lifted her chin, looking at him, a wry smile washing over her attractive face. Leaning to him, she did the one thing that both surprised him and made him stand in wonder. Kissing him on his cheek, she brushed her fingers against his own.

"Perhaps we could hold hands again someday Samuel.", she whispered.

When she placed the kiss on Sam's cheek it was a moment he recognized. As though he had witnessed the entire exchange the two of them had by the wagon. His awkwardness. His fumbling with finding just the right words to say. Her obvious infatuation from not only the other night at the theater but the way she looked at him now. And of course the open invitation to hold hands again. As though he was standing in a balcony watching that scene play out knowing exactly how it would end. The feelings he recognized. As though a memory resurfaced. Talking to his doctor about it would probably be best.

The hospital where he was a patient had significantly reduced its numbers. Hospital ships were now making daily runs across the Atlantic, returning American soldiers to their homeland. The English Channel became a non-stop highway of passenger liners with the same goal and ultimate destination. Returning England's boys back to their own families. Paris was beginning to slow down. Soldiers at every street corner became a rarity with only the unlucky few staying behind to rebuild the hundreds of country towns and villages devastated by the war.

"Well Samuel. That's really good news. It means you had a small memory released from whatever hold your mind had on it.", said his doctor.

Samuel listened, not saying a word.

"But also. I'm concerned. Too quickly could flood your consciousness with your past, whatever it may be. It could be overwhelming and too much to bear all at once, especially not really knowing where it will lead you. Go slow Sam. Really slow. When you have a memory, or even a feeling like you just experienced, don't dwell on it. Just accept it."

Samuel nodded, still silent.

"Samuel? What's wrong?", asked his doctor.

"Nothing is wrong doc. That's the problem. Everything is right. I'll be discharged soon, cleared to leave. But where? America? More than likely. But where? New York City? And do what? I know nobody. Here, at least, I know you, some of the staff around here. Ettienne and Monique…", Samuel said.

His doctor listened. "Ahhh, Monique."

"Yeah. Monique. I think I love her. No. No. I know I do. I'm falling for her. It feels right. And that feeling, I'm fairly certain I've felt before. There's an experience there that I just can't place.", Samuel replied.

The doctor reached for a pad of paper and a pencil and said, "Follow me Sam."

They walked together down the hall and into an office. Standing behind his desk Sam's doctor for the past eight weeks scribbled then ripped off the sheet of paper handing it to him. "This is your hospital discharge Samuel. You no longer need my care. The kind of care you need now I can not give you. But you know where to find it. You are in that process now. Go to her. She's your medicine. Whatever happens, happens. Don't fight the feelings. Don't fight the memories or try to analyze them for anything more than what they are. If, someday, and it's no guarantee this will happen, your memory of your former self may never return, but if it does, then that will be your time to start putting back together the puzzle that has been jumbled and mismatched."

Samuel took the discharge paper shaking the doctor's hand. "Thanks doc. I mean it. Thanks. I'll stay in touch. I'll drop by from time to time."

"The warm season is here Sam. Spring in Paris is lovely but I won't see it. I'm being transferred to Italy. There's a hospital there for invalids.", replied the doctor.

"Ahh well. It seems we both move on then. Best of luck to you doc. And who knows, our paths may very well cross again." replied Sam.

Outside the hospital Samuel found the bike that he used to get himself around the city. As he got on and began pedaling he couldn't help but think today had become the first day of a new beginning. His military discharge papers would be active any day now. He was in good health; had survived all the battles of the war. He was in the most beautiful city he had ever seen, had a job working for a family he adored and was falling in love, for perhaps the first time in his life. Everything did feel right as though it was all going in the direction it was supposed to be going.

When Samuel arrived at the market he immediately looked around for Monique. Leaning the bike against the side of the store, he went inside where he saw her father, Etienne, the kind and elderly man who not just took him in for recuperation but gave him the start at another life. Approaching the fatherly figure Samuel asked him the question that must be asked. Standing before him, hands clasped behind his back, in an attentive position as though he was addressing one of his commander officers, he chose his words.

"Sir. Excuse me Sir. I wanted to let you know that the hospital has discharged me and that I know longer am in need. Also, the Army will be releasing me from active duty soon. I'm not exactly sure what that means, nobody knowing where I…I mean, not knowing who I was before."

Ettienne listened, standing behind the counter holding a basket of cabbages that had just come in from the winter harvest.

"Samuel, my boy. I know what it is you are asking. Before you say more, the answer is yes. I will not accept anything but a yes from you. You may continue to work here. And you may stay here. You take my boy's room. It is yours now.", replied Etienne.

This was not what Samuel had expected, taking him by surprise.

"Sir. That is very generous of you. You have been far too kind. But of course I will not say no. There is something else though.", replied Samuel.

The old man listened inquisitively.

"I would like your permission to court your daughter. Monique. The theater last night was….right. I promise I will be honorable and I assure you nothing bad will ever happen to her.", said Samuel.

The old man simply smiled. "Ahhh, Samuel. I already know this as well." said Ettienne, patting him on the back and chuckling. "Of course. Of course. I will not say no and neither will you."

From behind a middle aisle, there came a small laugh followed by an enthusiastic "Oui". Both men, young and old, turned to see Monique with hand over her mouth, eyes gleaming.

"No time like the present.", stated Samuel, as he quickly went to her, taking her hand. "Sir. we'll be gone for the morning."

The old man simply smiled again saying to himself, "I know this too."

The two of them rode the bike to the outskirts of town. Samuel pedaling and Monique delicately balancing on the handlebars. Coming to a stop, Samuel pulled up to a partial broken split rail fence line where he leant the bike. Monique slid off, flattening her dress.

"We're here.",proclaimed Samuel.

Monique looked around. "Here? In this field?", she said in disbelief. "Monsieur Gagnon's cow pasture?"

Samuel smiled widely. "Yuh. Our first date. You're gonna love this.", he said excitedly.

Monique was skeptical but relished the time of just being with him, especially with her father's permission. They walked hand in hand, that feeling even stronger than the night before. Strolling through the pasture they stepped lightly and gingerly through the tall grasses, watching the ruts and mounds of a sometimes vegetable field, talking a little here and there, but mostly walking in silence. A small hillside became clear not far away.

"Over there. That's our destination.", said Samuel.

Monique only smiled, nodding in the direction.

As they climbed the hillside the ground changed. It was obvious the small hillside had never been rutted or rock picked for growing. Small outcroppings of visible stone could be seen through the much taller grasses than what they had just walked through across the field. With the sky blue with nary a cloud, they reached the top where a vast stretch of wild flowers awaited. Gourdon and Star Jasmine littered the hilltop.

"Usually, the boy will bring the girl flowers."Samuel broke the silence as Monique stood with an air of happiness. "But I couldn't decide on exactly the right kind. I've been told that Paris is beautiful in the springtime. Before I started working for your father, I used to walk here and sit up here. It reminded me of a ……place I had seen on a postcard. A hillside overlooking a village surrounded by open fields. I knew that spring would work it's magic here even then. So instead of bringing you flowers, I decided to bring you to them."

Samuel held her hand still, a little tighter, a little more reaffirming to his affection and intention.

"Monique. I love you.", said Samuel.

Monique nodded, at a loss for words, saying only, "Moi aussi."

28

Mary's Fatigue

Mary stood on the Pont Notre Dame over the Seine River, the magnificent Notre Dame Cathedral on the other side. After her arrival in Paris as a volunteer as part of the Allied War Relief, she had been assigned to the American Military Hospital as part of the ambulance corps. As the war wound down, more and more field hospitals were sending in the more mortally wounded soldiers. Soldiers who lost arms, legs, often both; their eyesight, hearing, and even sanity. She worked incredibly long hours, double shifts were the norm. She lived in a woman's dormitory not far away, so Pont Notre Dame became a destination. One that meant solitude and a time to take a breath. As her father was a doctor with high hopes his only daughter and child would someday follow in his footsteps, taking over the medical practice he built back home, Mary was accustomed to the blood, the pain, the loss of life. And as good as she was at her practice, 'gifted' according to the nurses she worked with, it was not the reason why she made the Atlantic crossing out of Boston Harbor. What she could not fix was the loss of love. Somewhere in Europe, Samuel was. She knew it. Despite no such name ever appearing on the wounded, dead or missing in action lists, she continued to feel his presence. So whenever she could, she would come to the bridge, in hopes to find Samuel again. To hear his voice, asking "Thinking of taking a swim?"

Reaching into her pocket, she took out one of the few photos she had of them together, taken not long before Samuel departed. A simple photo, he in uniform and she next to him, they holding hands in their special way; his index finger curled around her pinky. The bridge had lots of photos, and flowers, wreaths, and trinkets that lined the railings as it had become the memorial for the fallen and lost. Placing her photo with the hundreds and hundreds of others, she placed a single fingertip kiss to Samuel's image. "Someday Samuel. Someday." she whispered.

29

Faint Memory

Sam closed up the market for Etienne on a night that marked the closing of summer and the beginning of autumn temperatures. Locking the door and placing the key in his pants pocket, he decided to stroll through a park close to the Notre Dame Cathedral. Street lamps glowed, casting his shadow up and down the walkways and across grassy lawns littered with the closing colors of the warm season. This time in Paris was magnificent, he thought. The nighttime lights of the city cast soft, warm glows all around him as lingering aromas of small cafes and bakeries throughout the day held fast. Evening restaurants now opened with the hustle and bustle of early diners, as entirely new smells of fine, French foods wavered, exhilarating his senses. And the architecture of each building, with an Old World flair, gave him a feeling of wonder and amazement. A city he was just beginning to know, his mind was on only one thought, despite the massiveness of even Notre Dame looming in the near distance. Monique was all he could think about. There was an obvious attraction and even more so a very real connection the two had together. There was no denying it. But it was more than just her physical presence that kept him stunned and unable to think much of anything else. It was something that he didn't have the words to describe or, perhaps, to fully comprehend. A connection. Deep. Meaningful. Powerful. An unknown force drawing them both together. And because of his memory loss, he had no experience of making sense out of any of it. All he had was his name and his feelings for Monique and Paris itself.

Square Jean XXIII had become his destination when he didn't need to be at the market. Although his need to be at the market had greatly increased over the last week, since the theater. He found himself finding reasons why he needed to be there even when he didn't need to be there.

The evening commenced, setting a casual pace, enjoying the many Parisians as they strolled too, some sitting on park benches while others just seemed to hesitate in their step, stopping to point at this and that, various points of personal interests. This was his favorite. Just watching the people. They reminded him of something, perhaps another place, but just couldn't bring forth the recollection.

As he neared the gazebo, he eyed the young couple sitting on the bench where he often did. The spot gave a wonderful view of the Cathedral, with its towering spires reaching for Heaven itself it seemed. He stopped suddenly, shadowed under a tree, and just watched the couple. With very little movement from either of them, they seemed to be talking in a low, quiet tone, his arm around her shoulders, and her hand holding his. And like a heartbeat that skips, he felt it. He had seen this before. Been here before. Perhaps even had been the young man himself, before. The gazebo was the same, but different. Taking in the young lady now, he observed her more closely. Her raven hair that touched her shoulders, to her eyes that seemed to smile with delight at the man she was with and all that was around them. As his own hand reached for the tree to steady himself, he whispered one word, "Mary".

30

A Father's Wish

"I'll be leaving Monsieur Ettienne," said Samuel.

The elderly Frenchman looked at Samuel with surprise. "Leaving? But where? You are good here. You do a fine day's work. And my customers like you. You work hard. And you have won over my daughter.", replied Ettienne. "She likes your American accent. New England."

Samuel chuckled. "Hmmm. Now I know why she looks at me oddly. But, you see. I need to. I have a lot of thinking to do and honestly your daughter has become a distraction."

"Ahhh yes. I have seen how you both look at each other. It was the theater.", replied Ettienne with a wink. "The same happened with her mother and I."

"You and Monique have given me much inspiration and hope, Monsieur Ettienne. Though it pains me, and how much I want to stay, I fear this is something I must do. I had a life somewhere before …all of this. I have to find a way to remember who I am. Where did I come from? Who are my parents?" said Samuel.

As Samuel spoke, Ettienne listened, nodding with understanding. And as he placed a hand on Samuel's shoulder as a father would do to his son who has come to such a decision, the kindly old Frenchman embraced him then. A hug that was deep, meaningful, sympathetic and empathetic to his plight. When the old man parted, taking a small step back, he simply smiled, saying "Wait. Wait right here." and turned to go to the back room. After a few moments, moments that left Samuel standing alone amidst the shelves of merchandise that he himself placed over the course of the last several weeks, he could not help but think how fortunate he really was. Four months ago he walked out of an internal firestorm, an epitome of hell itself, deaf, blind, beaten and tattered and blackened, with filthy caked on mud, his uniform literally blown off his body, the only survivor of an entire regiment. And as he recouped in the field hospitals and later in Paris, watching other soldiers whom he did not know lay limbless and dying, he could not help but question why he lived while others lay mortally wounded for the rest of their own lives. That was a question he needed to answer, along with many others. To stay with Monique and her father would only prolong those answers and leave an empty space inside of him, perhaps for the rest of his life. The time was now. He was ready.

Ettienne returned with two boxes. One under each arm. Placing them on the counter, he slid them to Samuel. "Here. For you. They were my sons. May he rest in peace. You'll need clothes and we already know they will fit you. You wore his suit to the theater and I could not have been more proud."

Samuel, again, was speechless at the old man's generosity. After a brief pause to which he opened the box flaps, running his hand over shirts and trousers that were folded inside, he turned toward Ettienne, this time giving the old man a hug, with the same kindness and adoration as a son gives a father. "Thank you Sir. Again. Thank you. I will never forget this."

"I ask only one thing in return Samuel." replied Ettienne.

Hearing the old man say his name for the first time made his heart skip, he became ever more attentive.

"You take my daughter with you. To leave her here would be heartbreaking for her. Samuel, my son. She's in love with you. And I see how you look at her as well. It's obvious. There is a connection between the two of you that is undeniable. Let her go with you, wherever that will be. She will be of comfort in your discovery." said Ettienne.

Samuel did not know what to say. His eyes dropped to the floor, darting to and fro, then slowly he lifted his head, to lock his eyes on the old man's.

"Monsieur? I…I don't know what to say. I have no idea where I am going. Where I will end up. I have nothing. But for a few coins, a steel disc with my name on it, and a strong will to find who I may be. My future is uncertain." replied Samuel.

Ettienne turned slightly to look toward the staircase in the corner that led to the upstairs living quarters. "Your future is descending the stairs.", said the old man.

Samuel turned to see Monique. Instantly he was caught in her beauty. He knew then, he could not deny the old man's wish for he was correct. He loved her. He was in love with her and living without her was not an answer but a denial of happiness.

Monique smiled at the two of them. With her broken english in her native french accent, she simply said, "You two look as though you are plotting a plan to take over Kaiser Wilhelm's estate."

Neither man said a word, only looked to the other, with disguised grins that didn't really hide their conversation. "Ahhh, my daughter", said Ettienne. "You are just in time. You are going on a trip."

At that Monique looked to Samuel with questions in her eyes. And with a small tip of his head, pursed lips, he silently asked "Will you go?" to which Monique nodded, a smile breaking over her own face, as she skipped the last two steps, running across the store she had worked at for her entire life, and into Samuel's arms.

"Yes. Yes. Yes. Yes.", she replied excitedly. As they stood in the middle of the store, sealing their fate with a long, passionate kiss as only two lovers can give, Ettienne looked on with not only satisfaction but also with a permission. Slowly, he made his way around them both, passing the candy jars, the drawers of yarns and wools, past the shelves of ladies Parisian hats, and up the stairs. Once in the comfort of his own bedroom, he opened the bottom drawer of his dresser, pulled out a photo album, opened it, tracing his finger over the photos of he and his wife, where they were once young and full of love and passion and desire, like the two below him. Quietly saying to himself, "It is as it should be." Keeping the photo album open, he laid down, resting his head on the soft pillow, closing his eyes for the first time in a very long time with the knowledge his daughter would be alright.

31

Goodbye Samuel

Mary opened the letter. Running her finger along the crisp fold of the crinkled and pale yellow envelope, she slowly let loose the seal that was folded by Samuel so many miles apart and so many days before. Sitting in the gazebo adjacent to the Pont Notre Dame and the Seine, she was not alone. Parisians from up and down the river quai de Gesvres on the Rive Droite with the quai de la Corse on the Île de la Cité, mingled along the pathways, among the fragrant spring blooms that gave the City of Lights it's inept and infamous name. Only three years away from her home, the small mountain hamlet in northern New England, she felt her place in the tiny park and gazebo where she sat. Much the same as the tiny gazebo where she and Samuel would rendezvous on many a night. Things were familiar. Small children; moms and dads; ducks and geese; hands outstretched in feeding, their time together as family, friends, or lovers. Mary's heart skipped a moment at the thought of her and Samuels trysts they shared together. Moments she longed and panged for; to replace the pain and suffering, the mournful woes from men she did not know the names of.

With an expert and delicate manner that would have made her father proud, she gave to those in need the nourishment and medical attention, her hands soothing wounds, light or great, of the soldiers who will one day return to civilian life.

"My Dearest and Precious Mary", the letter opened with. Lifting her eyes, she became a little vulnerable to those around her. Nevertheless, with the curiosity for Samuel's wellbeing she braced herself with a little more ineptness, her back pressed against the gazebo bench.

"It's been far too long since the last time I wrote. Tomorrow will be a day that may not arrive. I'm not certain if this letter will even make it to you. The build up on the front lines is intense. Everyone can feel it. I've watched friends break from the pressure and the uncertainty they may never see another sunrise again. The battle that brews ahead is certain though. And I'm equally as scared. But I promise you Mary, whatever happens, I will find my way back to you. I promise. I need to go. Lots going on. All my love, Samuel."

Mary folded and creased the letter, like she has done a hundred or more times, slowly and carefully sliding it back into the envelope. Like she has done a hundred or more times. It was dated a year and three months ago. Samuels promised words the last he had written her. Taking a small breath, catching her emotions, she looked across the park to the many people coming and going. Some holding hands, others with children, a few by themselves, like herself.

"Goodbye Samuel", she whispered to herself. Standing and facing the direction of the hospital, Mary stepped down off the steps of the gazebo. "My love." her final words to the man who she held onto with hope and prayer that he was alive. With each step, she stepped closer to an unknown future. One which she accepted Samuel would not be a part of as they once dreamed.

32

Leaving Paris

The sun set over the Parisian autumn, once blooming with fragrances competing with the fine French cuisine that lined up and down the River Seine. Coming to the end of her nursing assignment at the hospital, Mary began longing for home. Going from six days and nights a week to only three she found herself drawn to the many squares and parks around Notre Dame. Strolling now, with her friend Claire, the two tired and drawn out nurses linked arm in arm as they walked quietly together. It was Claire who broke the silence.

"Stay with me.", she said with an obvious catch to her voice.

Stopping, Mary held both her hands in her own.

"Ohh, Claire you are a dear. We've shared everything together for the past two years. You know why I'm here and I've shared with you feelings I've not shared with another except for my Samuel. I have to go. To continue. Perhaps I will stay if I do not find him. I don't know. But if I do, it will be you I come to.", Mary replied with sympathetic eyes and a smile that endeared the two together as best friends thrown together in a turmoil of pain and suffering.

"Better days are ahead. I know it.", said Claire.

The two continued, their pace once again casual, their arms linked, the crisp, fall air filling their bodies, temporarily relieving and forgetting their jobs; of the constant, horrifying cries in the middle of a third shift night, from once upon a time soldiers who simply want to live again.

"There's a town not far from here. It's there I will begin. Work my way further away from the city. Samuel is a small town boy and its a village he will seek out. I feel his calling for home inside of me." said Mary.

Claire simply smiled and nodded. "I will go. With you. And we will find this boy."

The two laughed lightly, as their step improved like the lilt in their laugh.

"Well then. We will become inseparable." said Mary.

33

A New Way

Samuel and Monique settled into the tiny hamlet easily, without fail or flaw. They fell in love with the smallness of it all. From the cobble stoned streets to the tiny shops that lined either side. Ones that reminded Monique of her fathers own market. The people were rich, not in wealth, but with one another. They valued conversation, no matter the time of day, giving no never mind to how long it took out of their day. Time seemed to stop unlike the hustle and bustle of the City of Lights. The village itself, as though through some miracle, seemed to be little affected from the war, in contrast to the surrounding towns and countryside around it. Not big enough to be worth even a stop over it appeared. Though, after a few wanderings about, Samuel did notice some small signs. The public well was dried up, posted with a scrawling hand of red paint indicating it so. Overhearing a couple of town folk one day, Samuel learned the lake two miles away, which was the source for the ground water in a ten mile direction, had been so badly damaged with mortar fire the water source became altered. And of course there were the people themselves. Happy but poor. Subsisting as farmers, fields were destroyed and without water, crops and livestock they were doing nothing more than struggling to stay alive.

With a small purse of money from Etienne they were able to rent a three room cottage on the north side of the village. Close enough to walk to and from town, which they did a couple of times a week, but what was even more enjoyable were the pair of bikes they found in the shed covered with a tarp and littered with old hay and odds and ends. It took little effort to bring them back to pedaling condition again, what with a few squirts of oil along the chain.

"I do enjoy riding a bike." Samuel told Monique on one such trip to market. "I think I did a lot of riding when I was younger. It seems like I did."

"Father and me and mother would ride all over Paris together. My favorite were the parks along Notre Dame and the river." replied Monique.

"I think I'll pick up a few pencils at the store today. I still have plenty of paper in the journal the doctor gave me. I did say I should be writing down any little memory I may have, no matter how vague."

Monique rode along side of Samuel, smiling, the plain printed floral dress billowing in the breeze, while her long raven hair blew over her shoulders. It had been weeks since they left Paris, for the first time he felt settled down. For the first time, Samuel realized, he could stay here. With Monique.

"Race ya to the well." Samuel shouted.

Monique was taken by surprise, as she watched Samuel pedal away, thirty, forty, and quickly a hundred feet ahead of her.

Later in the day, when they returned to the cottage, their new home, Monique worked on sprucing up an outside garden area where it had once thrived with color. Samuel took this time to open his writing tablet. Reaching into his pocket for a pencil he felt the small metal disc that he always carried with him. A symbol of who he was, or once was. As he held the military disc between thumb and forefinger, the confusion he had was still very much real. "Samuel …Blood Type…" was all that was legible. The rest had been melted and deformed from the bombardment in the trenches. Laying it down in front of him, he began to write.

Leaning against the inside wall of the carriage house was my bicycle. A Royal Enfield with white wall tires and fenders and goose neck handlebars, it was dark blue in color and I called it George, after King George of England. It was one of my favorite things to do during the summers and I went everywhere with it. Daddy taught me to ride. Holding onto the back of the seat while loudly shouting "Pedal! Pedal! Pedal!" I'm not real sure why he had to shout so loudly. I suppose it was his excitement. And it was exciting. Learning to ride. The first time pedaling, without toppling over seconds after he let go, or slamming into the side of the carriage house or a rock wall. And when he had the confidence I would not, he allowed me to stretch my distance to down over the hill, which was another challenge on its own, learning how to use the coaster brake at just the right time with just the right amount of pressure to slow down. But I did learn and became an accomplished bicycle rider. I rode all around town. I used it to go on errands to the store for Daddy and to visit friends. I used it just for the sake of riding it when I had nothing better to do. At twelve years old George and I stretched our wings to explore for the first time, places I had before and places I had not, unchaperoned, completely by myself. And it felt wonderful. A sense of freedom I suppose but even more than that, a sense of being older, no longer a kid. Now, a young man who Daddy could trust, had faith in, knew I would be alright taking care of myself away from home.

Samuel put down the pencil. It struck him then. Away from home. That is exactly the way he had been living for the past couple of years. Away from home. What he and Monique were doing now, was building a home, a place he knew he must have had at one time but had no recollection. And for the first time, what he just wrote, the bicycle became his vehicle, the image of finding his home again. For the first time, writing became a tool and a map toward the destination he knew he must take.

Monique was very much a part of that destination. It was the wild abandonment that clung to them like a southern, summer heat on dampened sheets. The sheer wanting that drove them to be together, a yearning, from the setting of the sun, to the rising of a crested moon against cloudy or clear nighttime sky, to the rising of the next day where they relinquished themselves into the other, slaking a thirst as though dying from fulfillment.

It was the wild abandonment that redefined their wants and needs. Never before had they felt the yearning for desire. Never before had an impassioned and unbridled longing erupted a sexual bliss that gripped their loins like fantastical ecstasies of excitement. When he whispered, "I want you." she quivered, caught breath, her heart that never beat so fast. For his seduction was slow, sincere, silent, indulged with sensations that spoke in a language she did not know.

Coupled together under satiny sheets, the sounds of silence afterwards brought the wisdom of where they had been and where they were going; not amiss to them. Internal vibrations that delved from the moment, had both their minds in a synchronized dance; no orchestra, yet a music that was instinctively captured; a waltz that was tempted by a thousand generations before.

"Kiss me." she spoke. And of course he did. Following through her desire to feel his touch, his mouth taking hers, lips gliding like chocolate on silk. The map which he possessed of her body was exact, accurate, and true, as though he may have surveyed every angle, every inch, each hollow spot where the most sensitive of pleasures lingered; low moans that escaped her throat. He her lyric, and she his muse.

And so it was, and so it came to be. Whether in the silent, solitude of an orchard, the shore line of a foliage filled lake or pond, or the sanctuary of their bedroom, their wild abandonment for the other set the tone, theme, and novel between their wants and what would become their need for the other.

34

Learning to Write

She played on the swing with feet dangling, a young girl at age fifty three, hands firmly gripping the old rope as she gently rocked, a smooth motion, the same as once done some forty or more years ago.

The maple tree, in full fall color, has stood with said swing like the famed Gibraltar, changing colors year after year but never its stature. Weather worn and aged, the swing has waited almost a lifetime for this moment. Black and white photographs can be found across faded years in yellowed albums, of the girl when young now grown. An heirloom the swing has become and with feet dangling, hands firmly gripping the rope, the woman giggles with youthful joy and aged spirit.

A red orange leaf flutters to the ground.

We live our lives behind the masks we create. Masks that are worn at the most convenient of times and in the most austere circumstances. Hiding behind such, we suddenly don a boldness in character, without flaw, to dance our new found confidence in and out of new faces; to smile the dainty smile of someone everyone thought they knew in truth. Yet even that is not enough to secure our insecurities in the best of times. Behind the mask we create, smiles are facetious and false to the hindrances and crosses which we bear. Often as not, ones we never asked for, but inherited.

And so it came to be in the year nineteen hundred thirty five. The high country of Montana speckled the rolling grasslands with cattle five miles wide. Not a ranch within one hundred fifty miles of each other. Nothing less than three thousand head. He rode in on horseback on a morning smitten with the bite of the November cold. Alone. As though out of the folds of the hills themselves. A ghost from bygone days. I remember watching him. Out the frost paned window of my second floor bedroom. Just a child with a vivid imagination and an urge to know more of everything I took in. He instantly became a hero. Only later, the anti-hero of a dime store novel. I did not know that then.

He rode straight to the barn, as though knowing exactly where to go. Where to stay. Where to stow the tack. And emerged with bulging saddle bags across shoulders that appeared even broader than before. A giant of a man. My eyes bulged wide as he approached the house. My house. My sanctuary. My only sense of safety in all my ten years. Just then I heard the footsteps of others in the house. Voices, softly speaking, grew louder as they passed outside my own bedroom door. Footfalls scurrying and scuffing down the staircase. The same sounds during a holiday, like Christmas or a birthday.

Voices of my mother. Of my father. Of Jeannette, the only woman I knew who could read, write, do mathematics, sing, play the piano, ride horseback, plant a garden, pluck a chicken, wash soiled linen, my clothes, my parents clothes, bake an apple pie and sneak me a piece on a Sunday afternoon. Jeannette was my friend and playmate. So I hurriedly dressed myself in anxious anticipation and nervousness of the not knowing. Exiting my bedroom, I remember standing at the top of those stairs, looking down to the front door that opened fully; the cold November air billowing into our hall in invisible waves, as he stood before my mother and father, my mother embracing him tightly, and he shaking my fathers hand. The first time I met my uncle. Like a Tom Mix movie. Only I saved a dime, playing my role in my own house.

Later. Much older now. I learned my uncle was a scarred individual that may have sat tall in the saddle, but crouched low and shuddered himself at the sound of loud, unexpected noises. He heard voices. Telling him to "Wear the mask Stan. Wear a mask." They can't hurt you when you wear the mask.

35

Jogging the Memory

He sat on the wooden ladder back chair at the small desk in their bedroom. Monique was busy with a neighbor friend down the road. The small journal laid before him each sheet of paper blank, unused. Taking a long single breath, he picked up the pencil and began writing.

"The Art of Walking the Rails"

The iron rusted tracks stretched across the county line like the black top pavement that weaves in and out of the hollows and valleys, over hills and grassy green dales, both transporting its passengers to places near and far. One, weathered with red rusty flakes, the other pot marked and oily stained, signs of overuse by those moving along in their lives.

The young, old man tightened up the laces of his shoes as he placed each, one at a time, on the ancient rail. For he knew this course well. This path took many a journey down. Paralleling the former, he made ready for the pilgrimage he has always made every weekend afternoon for nearly forty-years. A childhood playground now turned into the halfway point. The point of no return; where you can only look back to where you came from and look ahead to where you want to go.

Placing each foot carefully on the slim rail, he found his balance, taking the first step. It was always the first step that held his concentration the most. Never the second, or third, or fourth or fifth. Always the first. For that first step to anywhere caused one to swallow hard, squint a little harder, breathe a little deeper just before lifting heel to toe; holding that first breath, until its release and then the second, realizing you are on your way.

As the iron rails grew accustomed under the soles of his feet, his thoughts drift to other notions. Autopilot takes over, with a dashing of ideas, a smattering of concerns, life's problems left unsolved. Each step on the rail is equally as important as the next, as he becomes so entranced with the simple act of walking, his mind becomes caught in a meditative moment of pure tranquility. Sights, sounds, smells around him blur into the Universal crevices of his mind, lost in a sojourn of wanderlust and happiness. For like the travelers before him, those commoners of Canterbury tales, the unbalanced forces of life's greatest demons can only be defeated by the sheer will of a balanced and concentrated effort to persevere and survive. With each step is another victory and reason to celebrate.

The rail bed below him, lurks thigh high with weeds. The weeds that reach up with their flora and fauna blades, attempting to distract, but failing always. For to slip, to waver, to become distracted by the smallest of challenges, will often lead to his stumble, the downward fall that is difficult to stop, falling into the pretend quicksand of his childhood days. Starting over again, when he has come so far, he knows it will be difficult. The forces of evil will try to cripple him. However, his eye has never left the spiritual guide that moves him forward. The angel that has the unspoken name only heard whispered on his lips and only a few know. So he does not fall. He is steadfast in his assurance and confidence that this day will end with yet another victory, another celebration to his own Becoming, as he carefully but majestically walks that thin line.

Samuel put down the pencil and read back what just came from his thoughts. "Hmmm. Apparently I enjoy walking a rail line too." he mumbled, closing the journal.

36

Waking

He was an early riser. He felt, in whatever life he had before coming to Europe to fight a war, he always had been. He often wondered if his parents worked a farm, cattle or horses or sheep, or crop, or all of it, and he was up before the sun to work along side them. He envisioned living near the ocean, his father a fisherman on a fishing schooner, and he working with him, slipping out of the early morning port. Being a soldier was not a part of that reasoning but merely an after effect of what was already a part of him. And so he slipped from the covers, taking one last glimpse of her. The night before, and the night before that, and before that, they exercised their youth with a voluptuous vigor, as they entwined arms and legs, embraced mouths, and held tight the other. Love was not something he easily grasped as the person he came to be, but if the feelings he felt as he watched her chest sigh and heave with each slumbering breath, than he felt a better man for it. "You're beautiful in the morning." he whispered softly.

Carefully and silently, as not to disturb her rest, he moved to the desk, sliding open the drawer to retrieve the journal. He opened to the first page, where he had wrote about the railroad tracks the night before. Re-reading those words, his words, he realized that writing his thoughts came easy for him. That using language, feelings of expressions, must have been something he had done in the past. It felt accurate. Again, picking up the same pencil from the night before, he put himself to the test.

"The Last Christmas

It snowed heavily the night before Christmas Eve. December twenty-third was cold, colder than expected even for a northern New England winter. Wind blown snow drifts billowed across the unpaved dirt road, piling up against the farm house to just above the window sills. Even with lamps the snow covering even the smallest of window light darkened the rooms of the house to a haunting grayness, casting shadows in the corners, creeping to the Christmas tree that stood in the living room. It would be his last Christmas. He knew it. My grandmother knew it. His parents knew it, his children knew it. The oldest boys drove through the storm the previous afternoon, arriving way ahead of the cold, wind, and snow. His parents, my great-grandparents, "Old Joe" and Suzie, arrived in old fashioned style, by sleigh driven by his two horses Ned and Molly.

The tree was cut out the back of the barn and dragged across the frozen pond to the house. The boys trimmed it, shortening it's stature, shaping it to perfection, perhaps the best looking tree they ever had. The younger kids, my dad and his sister, aptly nicknamed "sister" by him and the rest of the family, made cut out decorations, chaining colored paper together and folded snowflakes with fancy designs. The older women busied themselves in the kitchen. Keeping the wood stove stoked with oak and birch, baking the traditional pies, including his favorite, his wife's, my grandmothers' apple pie with the cross-crossed crust, which, ironically, was my favorite as well; selecting the preserves from the well stocked shelves in the root cellar: green beans, peas, corn, carrots, of course yellow squash, acorn, and blue Hubbard; beets, radishes, and turnips. All taken out of the garden through the course of the summer and summers before.

That morning Ned and Molly were again hitched as a team and harnessed to the packing roller, where "Old Joe", despite being near 80 and against Suzie's wishes, sat atop the wagon while his son "Jopey", Joe Jr. led the team down the road, one end to the other, packing the snow as packed as possible. All the men in the family worked for the road agents at different points in time, taking care of the roads around the mountainside, either widening, laying down gravel, digging drainage ditches, or trimming bush and trees.

That Christmas Eve was jubilant and jolly, to be both cliche and nostalgic. The boys brought cigars, while "Old Joe" brought a taste of the latest batch of dandelion wine. The younger kids sat around listening to old stories as the family laughed together about their lives. And as he stood posing with all those around him, his clothes a little looser than usual, his frame a little more gaunt than last year, his elation radiated to each and everyone who gathered around him. No need for tears on a Christmas Eve with such love and happiness.

Closing the journal, tucking it back into the desk drawer, he nodded to himself.

"You are writing love poems to me, yes?" came Moniques voice.

She laid on her side, one hand cupping the side of her head, her dark hair flowing and framing a smile that left him defenseless from the first moment he saw her.

"Actually. No. A grocery list." replied Samuel. "A good one too." he added.

Monique smiled coyly at him, her eyes and demeanor saying more in gesture and stature than he cared to admit, yet he was drawn to her, and like that moth to the candle flame, he found himself moving from the desk and back to bed beside her.

37

Finding Himself

"William? William! Come along boy, get those shoes on, we're all waiting for you." That was most always the way it went. It didn't matter if it was a Saturday morning like that morning, or a Sunday morning before heading to church, or a Monday morning gettin' up and ready for school, or any other weekday morning where going to school was part of the required routine, it was always "William?!" stated first as a hurried, inquiring tone, and then as a parental demand "William! Come along boy…!" His father could be the most patient person in the world at any other time, but not when his youngest son, Billy, was keeping the entire family waiting. Perhaps out of a handed down patience like their dad or just out of good raising, little Billy's older brothers were not only understanding but most of the time doted over their little brother. Robert especially. This would later change as their age gap saw "the boys",as they were known, to head off in different directions as they became of age to venture off, leaving little Billy and his only sister Margaret, three years younger, to hold that extra special relationship. It would be Margaret who would replace Robert making Billy the apple of his sister's eye and take up the role as doting sibling.

After less than an hour travel time, down the mountain which the family called home for three generations, through Lisbon and the village of Bath, past Swiftwater, and into the farm town of Haverhill, with it's vast acreage of cornfields and pasture, they arrived at the fairgrounds, parking near the stables that Ogantz Camp used for their horse and dairy cows. Raymond had been working odd jobs at the camp since his teen years, mostly caring for the trail horses and taking care of the other animals. His oldest boy Richard worked alongside him on those days, quickly getting a name for himself among the staff as the go to guy to fix anything that needed fixing. Some staff called him "Tink".

The family unloaded out of the car, Doris with little Margaret, while holding Billy's hand, and the boys with their Daddy, where they were heading to the horse stables. Roland and Robert were anxious to get to the dairy cow stables where they had been raising "Gertie", a black and white heifer they had been raising all year. Excited about winning for best livestock, they had practically already spent the $50 blue ribbon prize money.

Doris, or mom as she was called by the kids, except Billy and Margaret, they called her "Momma", had created a heritage quilt with Grammie, Suzie, the kids grandmother, and

Dottie, Raymond's brother's wife, along with her own sister, Lottie. The four women worked all year on the quilt, completing the last stitch only two weeks before the fair. They entered the quilt in the quilting contest sponsored by the Lyman Grange, with a hopeful first place earning of $30. Nobody outside their quilting circle had seen it yet, but they were known as the best quilters on the mountain. Doris also entered her raspberry preserves, where Dot entered perhaps her best rhubarb jam in years.

The family was well known around the area. The men for their hard work ethic. The patriarch of the family, "Old Joe" became the centerpiece for persistence, perseverance, and determination. The women for holding the fabric of the family together. The kids all did good in school, were kind, considerate, with the occasional mischief that young boys were expected to get into. With three generations of family all living less than a mile from one another, holidays saw large table spreads. Between farming, hunting, fishing, and working whatever jobs that would earn a few dollars, the family were more fortunate than most during those years. Raymond managed to always have tobacco for his pipe and Doris a couple of extra nickels for each of her boys when they did their weekly chores. Even little Billy would lend a hand, gathering the morning eggs, and once in a while, taking special aim with one eye closed, tossing an egg at the rooster that didn't like him much.

"Boys. Let's go boys. Time for a photograph."Raymond said as he gathered his family around the car, lifting Robert on the fender and Roland behind up on the running board, while Tink leaned near him, and Billy nestled between his legs and arms. Doris took her rightful place next to her husband, with her only daughter Margaret in her lap. The old car once again took them to a place that brought smiles and even a couple of ribbons for preserves. As the fall air became crisper, the leaves of color began to fall, so too did the family grow together for another year, covered by the tight stitching of a heritage quilt that would be passed on for generations to come.

8:30 am on a Saturday morning was not made to linger. Not in Lyman. It was made for a 9 year old boy and his grandmother walking the well worn pathway to the barn, some sort of basket or box in hand. Passing the clothesline where bed linens and curtains hung, a slight billow in the breeze even at that hour; past the old rabbit hutch no longer used, and passed the ducks that came waddling in from the pond only wanting one thing, somehow knowing we had bread in our hands. Grandmother and grandson would stop, crumbling bread and toss it to the flock, the kid tossing his small wadded balls into the water, making the ducks swim for their food.

"Will we get enough eggs for scrambled eggs Gram?", asked the kid as he continued to toss his bread into the water.

"Ohhh, I'm sure. With two or three left over for maybe a cake too.", she replied in response.

The kid said nothing, but tossed the entire piece of his bread into the water without breaking it apart, and hurried to the barn. They would never use what would be considered the front door, but always the wide side door. The one used for larger animals, like cows and hogs. Entering the barn, the immediate smell of hay and manure was present, like any barn, but also, the smell and air of a lifetime of use. To the left of the door as you entered was various items in disrepair, placed there years before, back when his own father and mother lived there when first married. And atop of that, boxes, bags, and various tools and buckets of the most oddest of assortments.

Ten stalls were to the right. Metal upright yokes made for the cattle that once made the barn a working farm. The concrete manure trough held moldy hay, a sign that such cattle hadn't occupied the barn for quite some time. On the other side of the yokes, were the wooden ladder steps leading to the loft nailed directly to the wall. At the end was a large stall that often held a hog or a sheep. To the right of that, the grain room, where bags of feed were stored. The chicken feed was kept here, and the chicken feed was exactly why the nine year old boy tossed away the bread. Filling up his bucket with grain out of the burlap Blue Seal bag, he opened up the next door, walking with his grandmother into a much wider area. With four additional stalls, this part of the barn, like the cow yokes, was seldom used anymore, except for, if looked carefully enough, holes could be seen scattered everywhere across the dirt floor. And if lucky, one of the many rabbits would pop up it's head or go diving into a burrow, it's tail the last to be seen.

"Your rabbits are getting fatter.", the grandmother said.

"I miss Trapper, but I know he likes it here.", said the boy.

Back in the spring, the boy and his father brought his 8 rabbits he had been raising in Littleton to his grandmother's. He still had 6 others in hutches that would one day make their way to the barn too.

Turning right, another door, and this one leading to the chicken room. Opening the door was always exciting, because you never really knew what to find on the other side. Either brooding chickens in their nest boxes or chickens flying at you all at once. It was here that a nine year old boy enjoyed the most. Reaching his hand under a chicken nesting, feeling it's warmth and the rounded and fragile treasure underneath was almost as much fun as opening a present not knowing what was inside.

The grandmother turned to him, "Now no throwing eggs at the hens. We need them all if you want breakfast and a cake."

"Ahhh, gram, I was little when I use to do that. I'm not little anymore." The kids' hand moved under a hen, removing an egg, placing it in the bucket he carried.

The grandmother chuckled as the two of them performed their chores. The barn may have been once filled to capacity with the livestock that kept the family busy years ago, but it never stopped being a place where lessons were learned through the natural cycle of understanding life and death. The kid is older now and the grandmother has passed, and the barn still stands, although much different in appearance. The kid often wonders if his parents broken stuff is still there, or if the stalls are still intact. Things that are broken have a place. The barn has good bones, and good bones will stand for a lifetime.

When Samuel had finished, exhausted, feeling hungover from the intoxicating effect of the pencil scratching against the paper, mid morning was leaning into early afternoon, rising without him even noticing. Looking to where he thought he would find Monique, he saw only the rumpled blankets.

"Whoa. Lost track of time on that one." he said to himself.

Standing, he went to the window to look out over the front lawn. And just like that he staggered back. Gripping the edge of the desk, he steadied himself, his heart palpitating what seemed a thousand beats a minute. He had done this before. Not here, but somewhere else. Looking out a window, over a covered porch, out across the stretch of lawn. And just like that he went back to a time of a younger man. A younger man in a hotel set atop a hillside overlooking a small town, much like the one he now lived.

"Samuel? Samuel, are you still writing? I'm going for a walk." came Monique's voice from the other room.

Regaining his composure and sense of consciousness, Samuel turned to the bedroom doorway.

"I'm here. Just finished. Be right down." he replied.

38

The Decision

"Where will you go Mary?", asked Claire. "Back home? Where is it again? New Hampshire? America? Or maybe become a debutante Parisian girl forever. You and I will have a flat, eat beignets in the park, continue with nursing, drink at all the clubs downtown, dancing with the cute boys."

Mary both rolled her eyes and laughed with her friend at such thoughts. The Paris hospital converted into a military hospital was again reverting back to civilian care. With the war officially over, the Treaty of Versailles signed and Germany defeated, soldiers shipped back to their homes, nursing staff was being cut back. And it was time to move on. She felt her work was complete. A nurse first and foremost, as her father had prepared her for since the time she could say the word nurse and had her helping in his office, to that ever real and ever strong pull she had inside of her to find Samuel. Always Samuel. Searching for him, asking every soldier she had contact with about him, raising her hopes time and time again, only to be let down, time and time again.

"It's time I go Claire. I've done all I can here. Samuel is alive out there. Somewhere. And it seems he remembers nothing of who he was or is. Whatever happened to him, whatever has taken his identity, he's out there. Wondering where he came from. And I'm the only person on this side of the Atlantic that can help him answer the questions he has.", Mary replied matter of fact.

"Oh Mary dear. You don't even know if that dear, dear boy is alive." stated Claire, as she kept pace with her friend down the parkway.

Mary grasped her friends hand then, squeezing tightly. The park across from the hospital had become a favorite destination for the two young women for the past eight months or more. They enjoyed the quiet yet brief escape from the pain and misery and suffering and sometimes death the hospital gave them everyday. And they enjoyed each other in their respite. Since the first day they discovered the park, they learned from the other they shared similar childhoods. Both had father's who are doctors and they both aspired to become like them one day. They both lost their mother's when very young, resembling their mother's fine features, and they both were only children, with no siblings. Perhaps even more in common, despite having grown up on opposite sides of an ocean, they both shared their first love experience. Not only through the usual ways of falling in love, but, like Samuel, Claire's Michel became a war casualty as well. But only Michel was killed in the early stages of the war, in a brief skirmish that will that go unwritten in history books or official reports. Unlike Mary, Claire had closure from Michel, whereas Mary was left with nothing but unanswered questions. Ones she simply needed to have answers to.

The early morning sun rose higher in the clear, spring sky, the park becoming more crowded with Parisians of all ages. With school still not resuming, children ran from tree to tree in games, while parents sat on benches, reading, watching, holding babies, sitting with family or friends. Where the park once saw uniformed soldiers strolling with sweethearts, now there were hardly any sightings of such uniforms, a sign life was beginning to become more predictable and routine, not the everyday fear of casualty lists, sirens, and food rationing.

"Where will you go Mary? I will go with you. I want to go with you. To find Samuel. To help.", said Claire, as she too gripped Mary's hand with a reassurance and delicate sense of security that Mary had grown accustomed to.

"Oh Claire. I could never ask that of you. What of your family? Your father? Surely you want to be with him?", replied Mary, as she stopped, turning to face her friend, holding both her hands in her own now.

"I will Mary. I will. But first, I help you. My father would understand. Our father's are alike you know. Your father understands why you had to come here. Mine will understand the same. It's who we are Mary. We are healers.", stated Claire soothingly.

Mary smiled. It's all she could do. She was both at a loss for words as much as she was stunned that someone she had not known for long had made such an impact and heartfelt connection with her. Tilting her head slightly with a playful look in her eyes, Mary turned, resuming their walk towards the hospital, swinging arms with gaiety.

39

Revealing Himself

Samuel held Monique's hand like he had a hundred times before, slipping his first finger arund her third. They had left Paris and her fathers market almost a year ago. The war had ended and life was beginning to feel like it once was according to Monique. For Samuel, he was in a constant state of confusion. His new found talent for writing stories, he discovered, had left him reeling. It seemed almost everything he wrote left him feeling as though they were actually memories of someone he had once been. He had never explained or shared his thoughts with Monique. Mostly because he wasn't quite sure what to make of them still but also because he didn't want to scare her. He loved her and he felt as though he was falling in love with her each and every day. If what was happening was he regaining his former self through the writing, than it was quite possible he was already married or had a family. That would be almost to much to have to deal with. So he decided to keep things to himself. For now.

"Samuel, what was your dream about last night?", she inquired as they walked along the open meadow that overlooked the small town.

"What? Why do you ask that?" Samuel replied, looking to her with curiosity.

"You talk in your sleep. You have been for the past couple of weeks. I think it's about the stories you have been writing. Some of it I can understand, but most of it is a jumble." she stated.

Stopping, Samuel let go of her hand, taking a few steps ahead of her. The morning was fresh, already the feel of the summer heat beginning to dampen brows and the back of necks. The meadow was alive with the yellow of canola and dandelions, a brilliance that could be seen for miles. A flock of sheep dotted the next hillside as Samuel turned to her.

"I didn't know I did. I … I've been having …dreams. And you are right. They all have to do with the stories. It's like I'm in a movie, an actor playing a part. Like … I've actually been to those places and done those things." Samuel told her. Looking out over the meadow and down into the town, he continued. "Monique. I'm scared. Scared of what I might find. I think whatever has happened to my mind, it's healing. My memories are coming back and in rapid fire. It's what all these stories are coming out so easily. And I'm scared that…that …" Samuel stopped, feeling a loss for words.

"Like you might be married? A husband and father? Samuel, I've thought of such things too. And it's true you might be. But you also might not be. I love you Samuel. But if you don't find out who you really are, where you came from, where home really is, than it's something you will always wonder about and someday, someday Samuel, you may even blame me." Monique confessed.

"Blame you? Ohhh, Monique I could never….I would never do that." Samuel told her soothingly as he wrapped his arms around her. Holding her close to his body, he whispered into her ear. "What if I don't want to find out? What if I like who I am right now? Would that be wrong?"

Monique didn't answer, her own arms embracing tighter was the only thing she could think of saying.

Samuel separated from the embrace, reaching into his pants pocket and sliding out a folded piece of paper.

"I wrote this early this morning. While you were still asleep. It's…it's about my father. I know it. A sled ride he brought me on.", Samuel said nervously.

Handing her the folded paper, Monique took it, looking to him. Unfolding it, she began reading. As she whispered the words to herself, she moved to the lone exposed rock, leaning against it. Samuel stood, hands in his pockets, watching, waiting for her response, trying to read her thoughts and expression.

Monique finished reading, folding the story. Handing it back to Samuel, she smiled. "That's a beautiful memory Samuel. And this … this is why you need to search for who you are. I'll be with you if you want. We can go to America. Start in New York, and follow your path no matter where it leads." Monique said comfortingly.

Samuel nodded taking the story from her, sliding it back into his pocket. "Alright. Alright. Let's do it then."

40

Wtih Child

"Samuel? I'm having a baby." were the words that he heard. Words that shocked him, scared him, and left him with uncertainty.

"What? I mean. You are? You're sure?" he asked with trembling voice.

"Yes. I'm sure. I am." Monique replied. "But Samuel. Don't let this stop you. You have to go. I'll go back to my fathers. You go to America. Find your family. Find yourself. Me and your son will be waiting for you."

Samuel swallowed hard, lost in so many thoughts his head ached, tiny beads of water forming on his brow. "My son? My son?" he thought. "My son."

For the rest of the day Samuel was nervous mixed with excitement for the future. For the first time, even with starting anew with Monique, finding their way together in a post war country, taking whatever jobs they both could find, did he even think of a future. For himself, Monique, and their son. Yet still, the void of where he came from, who is own family was, constantly plagued his mind. Monique was right, he knew. He had to find them. But now, with a baby on the way, and the very thought of marrying Monique, which admittedly he had been thinking of more and more as of late, he did have obligations here. Here, in this small village that they call home. In the two rooms which they rent over the bakery. The very word home they have uttered together since they arrived. They both felt it. They both wanted it. A fresh start. Together. And now raising their baby. Perhaps the writing was enough he thought. Perhaps its all that really matters. Putting down in words what comes to him. Though they may feel like experiences he remembered, nevertheless, they are stories that may prove to be worth continuing on. Someday, perhaps publishing them would be possible. Though not here. Not in this small remote part of France. America. New York. A new start. Opportunities to become a writer and be published. The three of them. That's where the future was.

Rushing home from the marketplace, he skipped stairs leading to their second floor home. "Monique? Monique? Monique? I know what we must do. Where are you? Come here." exclaimed Samuel with excitement. Not in the front room, he entered their bedroom but to no avail. "Now where is that girl?" he muttered. And as he slipped the last syllable from his lips, in she walked, carrying a basket of fresh cut flowers and a loaf of bread.

"Ohh, Samuel. I have great news. Sit down." she said happily.

"So do I. I know what we must do." he said. "But you first."

"I got a letter from my father. I told him he was going to be a Papa. He says it's the second greatest day in his life. The first holding me for the first time. He says…" Monique continued.

Samuel sat, listening patiently, happy for his her father. He would indeed be a kind and gentle Papa.

"And father says, or Papa, I think I should start calling him that now don't you? And Papa says that business is very good again. There's lots of money and people coming in these days. People reconstructing all of France. All of Europe. And he says it's time for him to slow down too. To be a Papa for us. So he's letting us take over the market. And we can live upstairs, just like he and mother did. Samuel, we can have a home of more than two rooms. In Paris!" Monique continued on but Samuel didn't really hear all of her words, just the enthusiasm in her voice. Since they moved, she missed her father immensely. He no idea what that feeling was like but he did recognize the sadness which she carried.

"Sounds…wonderful. When? When do we go?" he asked.

"Tomorrow?" she giggled with anxious anticipation.

"How about the end of the week at least. We'll need to settle the rent here and find a vehicle or at least a wagon to hire to move what things we do have. Unless you want to walk the entire way?" Samuel said teasingly trying hard to suppress what was his own exciting news.

"Ohhh, yes. Yes. Of course. The end of the week then. That will give me time to say goodbye to Isabel across the hall. She's been such a help and a dear to me you know." she said.

Samuel nodded taking note she did not mention of his need to find his own family. Back to Paris it will be.

The week didn't take long to end. Monique had said her goodbye's to the few friends and acquaintances she had made and Samuel as well. One of his friends who he helped cut wood for told him of an aunt who lived in Paris who might be able to him find some work if he needed it. And, he really wanted someone to pay her a visit.

Samuel secured an old ratty tatty ambulance to make the move. Barely able to start and not able to make more than ten miles per hour, it was nevertheless transportation that would hold the few possessions they had. They had traded labor for an old wooden table and two chairs; a rusted out bed frame that Samuel had found in a bombed building; a small chest of drawers which there was only one drawer.

And so they took to the road, needing to drive three hundred sixty five miles to reach the outskirts of Paris. Samuel figured at ten miles per hour it would take them a good three weeks providing they met a good downhill slope. Petrol would be an issue he knew. That would surely slow them down trying to find filling stations. But they were together. They had each other. And at this point, that's all Samuel really cared about.

41

Back To Paris

They arrived at Monique's fathers' store and house after five days of difficult driving and travel. Roadways were clogged with other families and individuals, all looking for something just a little bit better in a countryside devastated by the war. Most walked, a lucky few had the fortune of a horse or donkey wagon, one even a small cart pulled by a goat. In the cart were two small children holding with desperation all they possessed.

The old battle scarred ambulance they drove with what little they owned, to their fortune, decided to stop only a mile outside of Paris. Monique's father, Etienne, was able to procure a small horse and cart to retrieve their possessions. Returning back to Monique's home, they carried their belongings up the stairs, placing each piece haphazardly about the small five room apartment.

"It's good to have you back my daughter. The shop has not been the same without you. Makes me thinks the people were coming in to see you and not buy the bread and apples.", her father chuckled.

"Ohh Papa. Stop. Were here because you are. And because its the obvious choice. I'm having a baby Papa. Samuel and I will be parents in just seven months." replied Monique.

Samuel entered the room just then, holding the last of their things. Placing the tattered bag on the floor, he went to Monique's side, his arm around her waist.

"Monique, you said you'd wait to tell him together." Samuel said.

"I couldn't help it Samuel. It just came out." she replied.

The old man looked at each of the young kids.

"This news makes me weep with happiness. I'm so happy for you Monique. I only wish your mother were here to share your joy." he said.

"Papa. She's all around us. You taught me that. And if our baby is a girl she will be called after Momma. Sophia." Monique stated.

The old man swallowed, visibly shaken for a moment at the joy and love he felt for his daughter and now Samuel.

By the summer of nineteen twenty the City of Lights began bouncing back to its prewar days. Cafes and restaurants began opening their doors again, with outdoor dining up and down almost every Parisian street. Gentlemen once again dressed in suit and ties with spotlessly shined shoes and wearing panama hats and bowlers. Women tossed away the dresses they had worn out to colorless fades throughout the war, to buy off the rack dresses at fancy prices from exquisite Parisian shops. People mingled again, gathering at all hours, unafraid of air raid sirens. Personal wealth gained rapidly with the growing European economy. Jobs were abundant in the rebuilding of everything. From textiles to shoes; from farming to harvesting; from restaurants to hotel staffing. Europeans began traveling across borders for the first time in nearly six years. Train stations began running daily routes throughout France and across Europe.

The first few months Samuel and Monique concentrated in taking care of running Papa's marketplace. They learned quickly the small family market that had always been a part of Monique's life, was now a part of an entire city's. Etienne was already known across Paris for carrying the freshest of foods, particularly meats brought in from the farms and inspected himself, but now he was being called upon by the local farming community and industrial heads themselves. Etienne was known for his honesty, trustworthiness, and an interest in providing special services to his patrons before the war. People recognized that even more, choosing him to carry their goods in his store. It wasn't long before the small market became even smaller. Noticing the for rent sign in the store window next door, something that had been there for more than six months, Samuel talked Etienne into expanding. One side would be grocery, while the other clothing, textiles, marketable items that were being made in factories across Paris and beyond.

One quiet morning Samuel took the old ambulance he and Monique drove back from the countryside to pickup fresh vegetables from the other local farms they did business with for the market. Ettienne's store was doing well financially as was the entire city of Paris and most of Europe in general. Post war production was back and leaders of countries were once again negotiating trade agreements with one another. Economics were on the rise.

As he cut through the side streets he passed a new business with a 'grand opening' sign out front. "Kelly's Jewelers-Grand Opening-Specializing in Engagement, Wedding, and Anniversary Gifts". Before he knew it he found himself parked and getting out of the vehicle, crossing the road, and peering through the window. And there he saw it and there is when he felt it. The feeling struck him hard. One he had no real name for; just a feeling. So he acted on it and went inside. No more than a dozen minutes later, he walked out of the shop with a small black box in his hand and eighty-five dollars lighter in his wallet. As he started the ignition, the thought of what to actually do with it was all he could think about.

Radio began broadcasting again at all hours, a drastic change from the one or two hours in the morning and evening while the war raged. Monique always had the radio playing while working around the store. Now almost seven months pregnant she sashayed to the sounds of jazz on the turn handle phonograph. The sounds of Joe "King" Oliver, Louis Armstrong, and Bessie Smith played throughout the new shop, while the ladies of Paris came to shop for the latest and newest of European fashions. As Samuel worked both stores, going from one to the other three days a week, he could not help but stop and watch her when she was not looking. She was remarkably beautiful, and carrying his child. He would never had thought that possible when lying in a hospital bed, his body battered and beat while his mind struggled to comprehend even the simplest of things. He often wondered why he was spared the fate of his fellow friends and soldiers in his company. Why did he survive? He alone? As he watched who he knew someday would be his wife wait on customers and busy herself organizing merchandise along the many store racks, he would catch himself mumbling often a simple phrase of "beautiful in the morning" even in the afternoon or evening. It was a phrase that brought him happiness. One that gave him a purpose and meaning of why he lived. Seeing her dancing about to the radio, pregnant with gaiety, he could not think of a better place to be.

"Let's celebrate!" shouted Etienne.

Holding a bottle of red wine under one arm and three long stemmed glasses in his hand, he placed each on the dining table. "Tonight, we celebrate my daughter and Samuel and the soon to be birth of my grandson."

"Grandson?" asked Monique.

"Oh yes. Grandson. I have seen him as the first time I saw you my dear. It's certain." he said proudly.

Samuel entered the dining room just then. "Now Etienne. What on earth will you do if you have a grand daughter?" asked Samuel with a chuckle.

"Easy my boy. Love her as I did my wife and daughter." the old man replied with a hint of solemnity in his voice. "Ah, I need to look to dinner."

The old man exited, saying he needed to fix dinner. As Samuel and Monique stood together in the room, they were both silent. Peering about the room, Monique could not help but see all the little things that represented her mother. The china cabinet with the fine dinner plates she would use at Christmas and special celebrations. The last time on her twelfth birthday. The knick-knack porcelain figurines she collected of cats. And her most treasure piece, a small statue of Big Ben tower from her honeymoon in London with Etienne. It was the first time either of them had traveled out of France. Monique recalled how her mother would tell her she and her father were so young, with only the feelings they shared for the other to guide them. With train fare given to them from both their families, they traveled across the Channel for six days and seven nights, staying in a hotel across from the Thames River. She said it was the best six days she had ever had and the start of her new life.

Catching herself in the moment, she looked over at Samuel who was watching her with studying eyes.

"What?" she asked.

"Oh just noticing how beautiful you are in the morning." he replied.

"Samuel. It's mid afternoon." she stated.

"Seeing you, it's always morning to me." he replied back.

Re-entering the room just then, Etienne returned with plates and silverware, setting the table. "Sit, sit you two. I'll bring dinner out. I made your favorite Monique." the old man said as he pulled a chair out for her.

Shortly, he returned, carrying a pan of Coq au Vin with potatoes, carrots, and mushrooms. Placing the dinner in the middle of the table he served each of them then pouring glasses of wine.

"Tonight." he began, holding up his own wine glass. "tonight we celebrate my daughter and her wonderful Samuel. Samuel, I have known you for more than two years. You came to me from the hospital not knowing who you were or where you came from. You were a victim of war my boy and still are. But with the Good Lord's Grace, you have found a treasure in a sea of destruction. My daughter. And the two of you have created your own treasure, and so life moves on, and we find the happiness which we all once knew. Samuel. You have found a new life, with an old life yet to reveal itself. Perhaps someday it will. Monique. Your old life as my daughter will change, and a new life as a mother will begin. Together, the four of us will be a family."

Etienne stopped, a little choked up, sitting down slowly, taking an even slower sip of his wine. Samuel and Monique looked to each other, astonished at the old man's praise and acceptance. Clearing his throat, Samuel stood this time. "Well. This seems like a good of time as any. Sir. I have something to say. Or ask. Or….." Samuel stumbled for words at this point, taking a step near Monique, placing a hand on her shoulder. "Sir. Thank you. Your kindness is more then I could have ever, ever expected. And you are correct. I have found a treasure and a new life. And yes, perhaps someday my old life will reveal itself. But for now, there's nowhere I would rather be than right here, at this moment. I'm in love with your daughter and our baby to be and promise to be the best father. Not remembering my own father, Sir, you are the only person I can look to for that guidance. I pray I can do you proud." Samuel stated, clearing his throat, taking a sip of his wine. Turning to Monique, he reached in his pocket to take out a small sparkling ring laying it on the table. "Monique. My darling. This is something I should have done already. Marry me Monique? Soon.

Tomorrow? And I will love you every single day after until the vow I take comes to fruition." Samuel said with sincerity.

Monique, shocked and surprised, caught her breath, as her finger gently and lightly touched the ring, moving it slightly. The old man simply watched, he too surprised. Picking up the ring himself, Samuel took her hand, holding the ring over her finger. "Monique? Marry me." he said. All she could do is nod but then found her voice. "Yes. Yes. A thousand yes's." she said. Samuel slipped the ring on her finger. As he did so, Monique looked down the table to her father, seeing him with wet, watery eyes turned heavenward while whispering her mother's name, Sophia, over and over.

42

A New Home

Mary and Claire traveled throughout France, until coming to a small village in the southwest of Normandy. Like most places they visited there were still signs of the wars destruction across the countryside, however, even the smallest of french chateaus and villages were making a comeback, becoming thriving and economical again. People were happy for the first time in almost six years while an entire rebuilding process in all industries employed a population that was jubilant in going back to work.

Hearing of an orphanage that needed staff, the two found themselves knocking on their door. Almost immediately they were greeted by an older woman surrounded by three little ones, a boy and two girls, with another girl in her teen years just behind her.

"Good afternoon madam. My name is Mary and this is Claire. We were told that the orphanage here might be in need of assistance? We are both nurses." Mary said in greeting.

"Nurses? We have almost thirty children here, most no older than these little ones here", placing her hand on the five and six year old shoulders. "They are forever banging, tripping, and bloodying themselves. A nurse, two of them, would certainly be a blessing. I am Anna, Directress here." the older woman replied.

"We would need to have residence here as well if that's possible? Perhaps a trade for our services for room and meals?" Claire asked.

"That can certainly be agreed on my dear. And perhaps a little money as well. The church funds us of course, but folks are being more generous with their money these days, making more contributions at the altar", the old woman smiled, "so we have a little to share."

Mary and Claire both smiled and nodded. "Then we accept."

The orphanage was not large. With six bedrooms upstairs and four good size rooms downstairs, the home once belonged to the local constable and magistrate for the rural area. A stone cottage that sat in the back would be their domicile for as long as they cared to stay. Filled now with gardening tools, bicycles, only one which looked to be in good pedaling condition, an old coiled garden hose, several wooden tool boxes of various sizes filled with rusty and aged hand tools, broken furniture that never got fixed. Nevertheless, it would do.

"Not bad. I've seen worst." said Claire optimistically.

"Hmmmm. If you say so. I was hoping for perhaps a bathroom and tub." replied Mary.

With a big of a clang and bang and something or other falling from the wall, Claire declared, "Ah Ha. Found your bathtub." as she pulled out and half lifted a stainless steel wash basin large enough for one person. Looking at it with a bit of a grimace Mary squeaked out a "Oh joy" sarcastic reply.

But with effort and elbow grease along with a lot of vinegar and water, they both scrubbed and cleaned the walls, floors, washed the windows, and moved the items that were inside and attached with webs and dust outside, the stone cottage became much larger then anticipated. Mary was able to repair a broken table leg and wash it up to a presentable appearance, and Claire used the wash tub to soak the yellowed and dusty laced curtains back to their original whiteness. After the first day, they were able to stand back and see the possibilities.

"I think we have one more problem Mary." Claire said.

"Oh?" she replied.

"There's no beds. Where will we sleep?" Claire asked.

Mary blinked, thought, looked about the room. "Oh. You are right. Perhaps Anna will have a suggestion."

43

Beautiful In The Morning

Samuel awoke and rolled over to his side, where he placed his hand on Monique's belly, feeling their baby and his soon to be wife's soft slumbering breathing. Leaning just a little, he whispered to her ear, "You are so beautiful in the morning." A smiled crossed her mouth, her eyes fluttering just a little, as her hand grasped his own. Kissing her softly, Samuel sat up, dragging himself reluctantly out of bed, to dress. The night before still left him giddy with happiness as his and Monique's new life began to unfold, with the blessing from her father as the highest honor. As he buttoned his shirt, the ring which he slipped on her finger still in his vision, he stopped suddenly while staring out of the second story bedroom window that overlooked the cobblestone street below. The first signs of others awakening were present, as merchants began opening their doors for the days business. A little down the road from Ettienne's market, stood a four pillar hotel with double balconies at the first and second floors. Viewing the hotel, one that he had walked by and past perhaps a hundred or more times, his line of sight came upon the third story windows, in which he could clearly see a young man, perhaps fifteen or sixteen, sitting at a desk performing what appeared to be either reading or writing in a journal of some kind. This small minute moment struck him like thunder. He had seen this before. He was sure of it. The entirety of it all. A boy, writing, occasionally peering out of a hotel window to the street and town below. Like the sled ride memory he had months before, he quickly found his journal, pen and ink bottle, pulling up a chair next to the window, becoming the mirror image of the young man opposite. And like before the compelling force which drove him to put into words his inner most voice was far too much to resist, so he wrote.

"Tinkerville Store"

On a dusty paved road, traversing across a rolling countryside, around winding curves and over steep hillsides, past farmlands with vast meadows and pastures as far as the eye can see; and through the tiny hamlets with picturesque scenes taken out of what seemed like oil canvas paintings, and with both newly painted churches and paint peeling grange halls, small cemeteries set under old oaks, sets a lone country store with a single gas pump, faded and weathered but still the sign welcoming folks in. And those folks who do stop, the locals who have worked the land, harvested the crops, raised livestock for decades, some for centuries, know the tiny store as intimately as they do their own children. Pulling open the barn red screen door, a bell jingles, the hinges creak with time, as a dimly lit and well worn wide planked floor opens itself to all who enter. The counter is to the left, the coin register sets almost lonely, when nary a dime would fill its drawer. A red and white glass topped cooler with the words "Enjoy Coca-Cola", the iconic expression scrawled across the front and filled with green glass bottles of ice cold soda pop, tonic to some. The metal bottle cap remover hangs on the post near, a bucket of caps from those quenching their thirst, under it. If you turn to your right you'll see the wall of coolers, filled with deli meats, milk, cheeses, more soda pops, capped not twist off, and six packs of beer. There are only three aisles in the store. Two for the "necessities" as your mother would call them. Canned goods and loaves of bread, toilet paper and bathroom soap. The other aisle devoted to two shelves of penny candy. Candy for a penny. Rows and rows, a little kid's paradise to ponder over, as their dad samples the dill pickles and asks for a slice of the hanging smoked sausage; their mom picking up the necessities to last the week before the next trip. But perhaps the one thing that stands out about the store is its smell. That lived in smell; the smell of comings and goings by wayward strangers just passing through long enough to inquire about the weather and which road to take to get to the county courthouse. And to sample the dill pickles, smoked sausage, grab an apple out of the basket. That smell of neighbors who linger longer, swapping the latest gossip of so and so and how on Earth could the senior prom queen ever think of marrying the boy down the road. Conversations of upcoming fairs, grange hall meetings, town hall meetings, the price of corn this year, and who is handy with a wrench to do some handyman work. Fliers and notices hang on every available space outside and in. The tiny country store is not only a store to purchase this or that, but the very hub of a mountain community its inhabitants simply can not live without; economically, socially, politically, and all things in-between. One can not simply walk or ride on by. One must always stop, jingle the bell of the door, hear it's creak, smell that lived-in feel, sample the pickles, grab a Coke, popping the cap in the bottle opener adding to the bucket's collection, load up on penny candy, and trade a tall tale or two with the owner. The culture of such a place will become immersive and intuitive to a new found perspective. Simple things.

Samuel put the quill down, blowing on the page to dry the ink, then closing the journal. When he pushed himself away, standing to look about the room, Monique was no longer lying asleep, and the bed had been made. Glimpsing out the window, the street below was busy with traffic and people. Checking the clock on the wall, it read after noontime. It had happened again. He got lost in a memory that lingered about in his head. Only this time, there was a name of a place. Tinkerville. Immediately the implication of this name and place had a dramatic affect on him. For the first time in almost three years, he remembered a name from his past. Placing the lid on the ink pot, his hand trembled a little realizing the conversation that would eventually need to be made. But first, he was to become a husband and father soon, and this brought him back to the demeanor which he woke with. One carried over from the night before and one he knew would stay with him for the rest of his life.

44

The Wedding

"Our bridge. Notre Dame. It has to be." Monique answered.

"I agree. It's where we started before we even knew one another." replied Samuel in return.

"Papa will want to invite all of his friends. And I have aunts and uncles and cousins that will be there. And I will invite some friends from school. And ..." continued Monique.

Samuel listened on but couldn't help but think he had no family. Absolutely no one who would be there. Monique's family is all he had. But he was content with that. He knew it was something he had no control over.

"...and my cousins little girl will be the flower girl and ..." said Monique excitedly.

A worried look encompassed his face suddenly. "What? What is wrong Samuel? Do you change your mind?" Monique inquired with a concerned tone.

Samuel moved to the window where he looked out over the street below. For the past two years he had been working at the market where Monique and her father were the only two people who really knew his story. Of his lost identity. Of his memory loss. Of who he was not. The people who shopped at the market, those who lived in the neighborhood he had come to recognize and establish relationships with, but they did not know who he really was. Who is family was, where they came from. All they presumed was he was an American soldier who decided to stay in Paris and fell in love. There was no reason to give a last name or talk about his past. Turning to her, he told her with anxiety in his voice. "I have no last name to give you. How can we get married? The minister will want to know."

Monique had not thought of this either, immediately understanding his concern. "You are right. This has never come up before. There was no need. But..." she continued, reclaiming her composure. "...but, why can't you choose a name? Choose a last name yourself."

Samuel looked to her with an astonishing expression. "Brilliant idea! Yeah. Yeah. Why can't I?" He thought a moment. Then turned to her. "Waterman" he said. "My last name will be Waterman."

That night they gave her father the news. He laughed with delight but did not cry with joy. That had come a few nights before. Instead, he simply rose from his chair, hugging them both. "I am a happy man." was all he could say. He left them both, ascending the stairs to his bedroom, where he softly closed the door.

They stood on the bridge a few days later, he in the suit her father had given to him the night of the theater, belonging to his son. And she in a dress of white, modest and shapely, with fresh cut flowers in hand. They exchanged their vows, and listened carefully to the words and bible verses the priest recited. It was mid morning on a cloudless October day. A crisp yet warm Parisian fall where the people took their respites out of doors as much as possible before the colder weather set in. Moniques family attended. Both her father and mothers brothers and sisters with their children. Tears were shed and joyful laughter ensued. And of course others who happened to be on the bridge that morning, they too stopped to watch the age old exchange of promises followed by the 'I Do'. As Samuel and Monique faced the priest, his back against the river below, the glorious Eiffel Tower looming in the horizon, they both felt the giddiness of standing together as well as being awe struck of their day actually happening. The Bridge de Notre Dame held an important role in their lives, for it not only connected their lives together, but, for Samuel, represented the one place he could always find reflection and solace while he was a patient at the hospital. Here was where he could reflect on who he was, and who he wanted to be. Being surrounded with photos of soldiers and families, the love and loss was everywhere, as symbolic to both he and Monique as it was for countless others. So just before they committed themselves to the other by saying "I Do", the photo of himself that had been their for so long became visible and apparent when the priest shifted his stance just a little. And there it was. It was he. In uniform, standing close to a young woman, both of them no older than eighteen or nineteen. They were holding hands standing in a white gazebo. Moniques eyes went wide, as she looked to the photo then to Samuel, and back again. Staying composed, they committed themselves to the other.

"Samuel…" began the minister. Samuel leaned in to whisper to him, stopping him short. "Anderson" he whispered. The minister looked at him with surprise and bewilderment, but continued despite the sudden change in name.

"Samuel Anderson, do you take this woman to be your lawfully wedded wife?"

"I Do's" were said, they kissed, held each others hand, his index finger curled around her pinky, then turned and presented themselves to their family. For the first time, Samuel wept and Monique clung to him tightly. They became husband and wife, a future awaiting them. A future they both knew would be fraught with challenges and the unknown. For on that morning, Samuel's past collided with that future. Mr. and Mrs. Samuel Anderson had found one another and they had found himself at the exact same moment.

45

The Preparation

"We have to file immigration papers." stated Samuel to Monique and her father as the three sat at the dinner table. "From what I was told it's a simple enough process. You just need to be able to read write a little English. You will certainly be able to pass that test my dear. But myself on the other hand, it may prove more difficult."

"Why is that? You have a last name." asked Monique as her father dished out servings of stew from the pot in the center.

"That is true. However, the man at the consulate's office also said, though it was more than obvious I was American, but with no identifying papers, and no trace of my military records, it's going to be problematic." Samuel replied.

Monique placed her hand over his on the table. Ettienne then sat down, looked to Samuel saying, "Your army will have your papers. Find them and they will direct you. They keep everything."

Both Samuel and Monique nodded to the old man. Surely it could not be as simple as that.

The next day they went back to the immigration office. It was a different person from before that Samuel spoke to. "I'm in need of some information. I have booked passage on the passenger liner Chantilly departing from Saint-Nazaire. We leave on the fourteenth of March."

The clerk, a small man who wore wire framed glasses, sat behind his desk that made him look even smaller. "One minute please." he said. Turning and reaching behind him on a shelf, he pulled out a black ledger book, opening it and flipping pages.

"You speak English? I mean, you are American?" Samuel asked.

The clerk looked up. "Yes. Yes, that's right. Born in Quincy, Massachusetts. Got pulled into the war, wounded, did some time at the soldiers hospital here in Paris and never left. I mean, it's Paris right? Why would one leave?"

"The soldiers hospital? I was there too. For months actually." Samuel replied.

"I knew I recognized a New England accent. It's not Massachusetts. Certainly not Maine. I'd guess Vermont or New Hampshire. Northern parts I would guess. But yeah buddy, thousands passed through that hospital." the clerk said looking up at him then repeating himself. "Thousands" this time his tone changed. Melancholy in resonance.

Running his finger down a page he found what he was looking for. "Yes. Yes. It's here. Passenger ship Chantilly as you said. Leaving Saint-Naizaire on the fourteenth of March." the clerk read. "Oh. Now this is interesting. It's docking in New York, so you'll be going through Ellis Island of course. But after it's anchoring in Quincy. If you are heading back home, its easier to get there through the north shore than up through New York."

Closing the book and replacing it on the shelf, he seemed to slip that small piece of information away somewhere in his head. "Now. What was it you needed?" he asked.

"Any idea how I would contact the Army?" Samuel asked.

"So you are he. I heard about you. Lots of us have. The guy who fought for nothing we use to call you at the hospital. Men who came in and left all talked about you. Your story even reached the newspapers in America." the clerk told him.

Samuel sat in stunned silence. The clerk continued. "We all felt real bad for you. It's one thing to be wounded, its another to be wounded with your buddies you fought with, grown close to, but its a total different story when you have no one. Absolutely no one who knows you and you don't even know yourself. Totally alone."

Samuel nodded solemnly, his head tilted down to the floor. He had not thought of those days at the hospital for a long, long time. It seemed there was no reason to. He fell in love, and that's what he concentrated on, and put all of his strength behind. Without Monique and her father, he would still be lost.

"Look buddy..." the clerk began, writing down an address. "Go here. It's the New York recruiting office. Someone there will be able to help you." Ripping out the paper from the notebook he handed it to him. "They will be able to direct you to your hometown and next of kin."

Taking the paper, he read it. "Thanks" was all he could say. "Thanks." he said again.

"And buddy. My name is Carl. Carl Monroe. Wait a moment. Wait right there. I'll be right back." Carl said.

Samuel waited for what seemed like a long time, thinking about where this piece of paper may take him. When Carl came back he held under his arm a small paper bag. Setting it on the table he opened it. "I would like you to do me a favor. When you depart the ship in New York, more than likely you will find passage to Boston. Lynn is not far from Boston. That's where she and my mom live. Would you, I mean, could you deliver this to my parents? Let them know I'm alive. I'm alright. Where I am and what I'm doing?"

Sliding the bag over to him Samuel peeked inside. "It's a doll. I know, I know. I've heard all the jokes. My little sister gave it to me before I left. For good luck and all. I carried it with me in my pack all across Europe and into Germany when we crossed the Rheine. Find them. Give it back to her. The address is in the bag."

"Alright. Alright Carl. I will gladly do that. And, by the way, your story is just as good as mine. They should be talking about you too." Samuel replied.

They both stood, shaking hands. Even laughing just a little. Samuel walked in thirty minutes ago not expecting a lot of help, but walked out with a map and a doll that spoke volumes about the place he was going. As he stepped out the door of the immigration building, he laughed a little to himself, clutching the brown paper bag under one arm, while the address to the army recruiting office in his pocket over his heart.

46

The Tired and Weary

The morning sun cast its rays across the white crests of the early morning tide, as the ship sailed into New York harbor. The ocean seemed to shout with each slap against the hull as though to say "welcome, welcome. depart and start anew." Samuel and Monique and baby Joseph, yet unborn, stood on the fore deck, like a thousand others, as the sky scraping buildings became ever larger and closer. Thousands, from all across Europe, stood on board the steamer ship that morning with the same hopes, dreams, and prayers for betterment. None had any idea what the future would bring. But if life could be fulfilled here, with good jobs and opportunities, than the long voyage across the Atlantic would be well worth it. For Samuel and Monique, they were willing to risk their previous life in Paris for it. And if Samuel did find what he was searching for, then all the better. No matter what he would find, they promised one another their love and family were of importance to protect. Even if that meant Samuel had another family somewhere in America, for they both knew that was highly possible.

It seemed like forever for the ship to properly dock securely. Longer still for the gangplanks to be lowered for departure. And still longer to find themselves descending to the dockside, as throngs of other immigrants huddled and squeezed each other into a compact mass of human bodies all scrambling to find the exit. With British accents, French, Italian, what sounded like Norwegian, and a smattering of others they did not recognize, they quickly understood why America was called 'the melting pot' of the world.

Monique placed her hand on her pregnant belly to caress baby Joseph, while Samuel carried the two bags which held all their possessions. With each small step, shoulder to shoulder jostling, and very little conversation with others, they slowly approached the gang plank that would lead them to a new life. Others who disembarked from a place of hardship in their lives, dressed modestly, some wearing layers of clothing to free space in any bags they carried; children grasping tightly onto treasured playthings: dolls or toy cars. Some carried framed portraits under their arms. Perhaps relatives from long ago, preserving their memory and heritage, while others simply carried only themselves. No luggage, no one, nobody. With a bag under one arm and clutching another, a small brown paper bag with a doll nestled inside, his other hand stayed close to his jacket pocket where their immigration papers filed in Paris were folded in an envelope and the address to the army recruiting office.

The metaphor was not lost on Samuel that figuratively and quite literally he would hopefully find an entirely different person than the one he knew he was. With a pregnant wife no less, was not just worrisome, for the amount of responsibility, he knew, would at times be overbearing. Before leaving, he had found possible work in upstate New York and across the northern parts of Vermont and New Hampshire. There were large hotels there that were hiring for all positions. Vacationers across the country were escaping to the northern New England regions for skiing in the winter months and all that the summer time offered, and with almost guaranteed work, it seemed like an obvious destination. However, he made a promise to Carl. First, he and Monique would need to find their way to Quincy and the Boston area. From there, he knew, he could make his way further north where the hotels were.

"It looks like from Quincy we make our way to Springfiled." Samuel said studying and tracing his finger along the Boston and Maine railroad map. "That's about a hundred miles it says."

"How will we get there?" asked Monique as she sorted out their clothes from the suitcases.

They found a hotel to stay in for the night not far from the harbor, along with many others. The amount of people entering the country was astounding. More people shoulder to shoulder than either of them had ever seen before. Even Paris during the seasonal busy time was not this crowded. The streets were busy, noisy, and dirty. It seemed people didn't talk to one another, but shouted instead. Even in conversation, standing face to face.

"I'm sure there's a motorcar we could hire. We have eighty-six dollars left. We'll travel as far north as it takes us." Samuel replied. Looking over to her, he noticed her lying on the bed with her hand on the baby. "How's the baby?"

"Awake" she said with a giggle. "He moves around a lot and getting older by the day. Almost seven and a half months." she continued with astonishment.

"Mmmm, don't remind me." Samuel said giggling too as he rubbed his hand over her belly. "We passed that little outdoor market just around the corner. I'll go and find some dinner. You wait here. There's way too many people crowded together and I don't want to take the needless chance of you getting bumped and prodded." stated Samuel. "Keep the door locked and don't open it for anyone."

"Fine with me. I'm not exactly thrilled about this area anyway." Monique replied with a distasteful tone.

Samuel counted out five dollars, folding the bills into a small leather pouch and shoving it deep into his pocket. Leaning to her he kissed softly on the brow. "I'll be back soon. Hot sandwiches and a cold drink." Monique smiled to him rolled to her side and closed her eyes.

The open market around the corner was less busy than when they first walked by on the way to the hotel. Although he agreed with Monique's opinion of how crowded and dirty it was, it still wasn't as bad as what he was expecting. The stories he had heard about immigrants coming to America were very concerning. Bringing a seven month pregnant wife to a foreign country where you knew nobody was constantly on his mind. The amount of responsibility he knew he was facing raced his heart, needing to step away from things. Even before they left and while aboard the steamer for ten days, he often found himself finding a corner to regain his composure as quietly as he could, especially without Monique realizing. He never left her side, except for now, but knowing she was safe behind a locked door in a crowded city gave him some comfort.

Approaching a table where the line was shorter than the others, he stood behind one other man who was in full conversation with the man preparing some kind of a sandwich.

"I tell ya, jobs are getting scarce these days. I just got hired onto the railroad only two weeks ago. It's a decent job. I enjoy meeting different folks." the man said. Dressed in suspended trousers and a shirt that looked two sizes to big for him and hadn't seen a good washing in a few days, he continued. "But if the news is true, the B&M abandoning the northern route, including the western tracks down here to New York City…without the Boston and Maine making daily routes up to New Hampshire and Maine, it's going to put a lot of folks out of work and not just those working for the railroad company."

The man behind the table continued preparing the man's lunch, chopping up lettuce and onions and slices of tomato. "Hmmm. Don't know much about the railroad. I have no business or relatives who live up that way in New Hampshire or Maine or Vermont. I tend to my business here and that's enough for me."

"Well then Sir. Let me ask you. Is the majority of your business from people who live around here?" he asked.

"Some. On some days. Depends. The winter is slower than the summer. I see faces I've never seen before more in the summer."

"There ya go. Those are the folks who travel the train down from the northern parts, as far up as Quebec." the man Samuel stood behind explained. "Therefore the railroad maybe disappearing does effect you."

"Hmmm. We'll see. Until then, that's a buck and a dime for the sandwich." said the man.

Reaching into his pocket and handing him the amount of money he passed a final word. "Good luck to you then. And thank you." Turning, he almost bumped into Samuel who perhaps was standing a little to close. "Ahh, excuse me pal." he said, as he began to step around him.

"Wait. I overheard your discussion. Could I pick up a train that goes all the way up to northern New Hampshire or Maine from here?" Samuel asked.

"Nah. There's a line down, but that train heads back over to the Boston area from here. Now, from Boston, that train is still running, for now anyway. Like I said, if the news is true, not for much longer. Those railroad tycoons follow the money and not the people. They don't care where they go as long as they're paying." said the man to Samuel.

"I see." Samuel replied, stopping to think about this new information, then added. "And where's the train depot from here?" he asked.

"A few blocks over. Perhaps five or is it six? About a forty-five minute walk anyway." he explained.

"Thank you kindly." said Samuel.

"No problem. And, order the liverwurst. It's the best around." said the man.

Stepping up to the table Samuel ordered two liverwurst sandwiches and a jar of pickles.

47

Hello and Goodbye

The duplex Claudia and Mary rented in the small French village of Senlis, some sixty miles from Paris. With old world and well worn narrow, cobble stoned paved streets, the tiny village bolstered two and three floored buildings. The stone work watering basin at the center of the village, an ancient structure once used as a public gathering place for water as well as for live stock to drink from, became the villages icon, setting it apart from other area villages. Rows of flowering pots lined the streets, each merchant or home fixing the pots. The flowering colors in the spring and throughout the summer French months, led a traveler down the roads with an air of gaiety in their step such was the charm. A sure sign the war in Europe was indeed over.

Mary and Claire rented an old stone farmhouse only a few minutes walk to the market. With weathered stone walls lining one side and around the rear of the house, an equally sized barn stood, once housing the sheep, goats, and cattle. With some repairs and mending needed, Claire and Mary set out right away to make it their own. From pulling weeds from between the inlaid stone pathway to the front door, to mixing mortar to repair cracks in the walls, to straitening and shoring up crooked shutters on the windows. The orphanage itself was adjacent, perhaps fifty or so yards away. A squared off brick building with two stories with floor to ceiling windows, wonderful for the natural light of the morning and early evening, it provided comfort and security and a sense of home for fourteen youths, ages four to soon to be seventeen. Claire and Mary exchanged their services to care for the children for the rent on the cottage as well as a small monetary sum for living expenses. The two of them began falling into a daily routine that held for them both the happiness of being around the children and providing them care and comfort and the camaraderie they found in each other. Claire had no immediate family, only an aunt and uncle, she last heard from in London, they escaping the French bombardments early in the war. For Mary, her search for Samuel grew hopeless day by day. Always on her mind, she stopped nothing short of asking shopkeepers and civil servants and the occasional soldier, still active duty or discharged, of his possible whereabouts. Nothing ever grew from her efforts. It was as though he simply disappeared. And the more those times presented themselves, looking into the eyes of those she asked and seeing their genuine and sincere despair for her, the more that hopelessness grew inside of her. She began resigning herself that Samuel was just one of hundreds of thousands of others who were missing in action. If not for Claire and the orphanage, she would sink into total despair, for her heart still very much belonged to Samuel. Their relationship seemed only a short time ago, when their laughter on the carousel and their time at the gazebo were the only things that mattered. In only five years their entire lives were held in limbo and sorrow. Her yearning and lost heart became evident to everyone on a crisp, fall day, not unlike other fall days in the north of France, but with the war being newly ended this fall season seemed to be especially jubilant for everyone. Especially for a young man who strolled into the village carrying nothing more than a rucksack and leading a burro with one satchel and a ladder back chair while whistling whimsically as he smiled and nodded and greeted those who gazed curiously at the young man.

Claire and Mary were busy sprucing up the yard and house on a Saturday morning when their lives would unknowingly change. Dressed simply, he wore a light blue buttoned down, over sized cotton shirt that had not seen a proper washing for quite some time, paired with brown pants with rips at the knees and tattered at the bottom cuffs. His shoes were worn through, yet this seemed not to bother the gaiety in his step. With dark brown curly hair that rested just at the tops of his shoulders, hazel green eyes, and dimples at the corners of his mouth, Claire turned to Mary, in sudden exhalation.

"Mary? Mary? Who is that?" she said catching her breath and gasping.

"Claire! Are you staring? Are you…Ohhh my. You are. You're staring and eye balling that poor boy." Mary replied.

"Yes. Yes I am. And you should be too. He's the most handsomest man I've ever put my eyes on." Mary exclaimed.

Looking perhaps more closely after Claire's declaration, Mary said, "Well. He's alright. I mean….alright fine. Yes. He is. I must agree with you."

"A walking Adonis. I bet he's from Greece. Walked all this way in search of his fortune." Claire said.

"Or, by his appearance, he's hungry and tired." Mary stated.

"Well. That's it then. He must be invited in." said Claire as she lurched out the front door, crossing the front yard, to introduce herself in the middle of the road.

Smoothing her dress, she walked with hurried step, standing in front of him as he approached. To anyone watching it would appear she was not merely introducing herself but actually blocking his pathway.

"Ohhh. Well hello there." Claire managed to utter with a nervous tone.

The young man stopped, lifted a brow slightly, as he switched hands with the reins, looking first behind him, then to the cottage and farm, glancing at the orphanage itself, then finally to Claire.

"Hello?" he said.

Claire stood there in silence, shifting her weight from foot to foot.

"Hello?" he said again.

"Yes. Hello." she repeated.

"Well, now that we have the hello's out of the way, could you kindly tell me if this is the village of Senlis?" he asked.

"Ohh, yes. Yes it is. My name is Claire and I work here at the orphanage." she said as she pointed over her shoulder.

He glanced again at the orphanage, seeing for the first time the sign that read "American Red Cross Orphanage. Where Soldiers Adopt Those Who Are In Need".

Nodding again he said, "Hmmmm, perhaps this is exactly the place I was hoping for. You say you work here? Are you the director by chance?"

"Ohh no no. That would be Ms. Edith. She's at the residence now. I'm one of the nurses. My friend Mary...." turning Claire looked to their cottage. "...she's the one peeking out the window at us....we were both nurses during the war, working in Paris at the soldiers hospital. And now here we are."

"I see. Well. I'm looking for work as well. Perhaps the orphanage could use a handyman? I can do almost everything. And, I have a friend who works here." he said, winking to her.

Claire was caught off guard at this wink stating, "Excuse me? Did you ...did you just do what I think you did to me?"

"Ohhh, absolutely. See. I'll do it again." he said with a chuckle, and with that winked to her again.

"Oh my. You are...you ...." she began, then stopped herself.

"A flirt? The answer is yes. I am. Most women won't admit it, but they rather like it. As you do. I can tell."

Claire lifted her eyes to him briefly then turned, looking to Mary who was still peering out the window. Turning, she walked briskly back to the cottage without even saying goodbye.

Watching her, laughing hard, he shouted back to her, "My name is Alex. Miss Claire."

Gathering the reins again, he jerked the burrow forward, moving toward the orphanage.

"Well that was an interesting little display." said Mary whimsically.

"What was? What? Oh. That? He's just a silly man who doesn't know where he's going." she replied.

"Oh. I'd say he knows exactly where he's going." Mary giggled.

Claire blushed. Deeply. Both cheeks. "Claire. You're blushing."

"Am not. I mean, well, perhaps a little." Claire giggled in return. "But can you blame me?"

"What is his name again?" asked Mary.

"Alexander." Claire replied.

"Ahhh. You see. You're blushing even more now."

The rest of the day left Claire almost useless. She lost her mind and head in thinking about Alexander. When washing the windows, it took her more than two hours just to do one. As Mary watched her, she couldn't help but stifle a laugh at watching her attempt to wash the same window four different times. Watching her though, brought back her own yearnings for Samuel all over again. What she thought for sure were feelings that had withered away a long time ago, were still there just under the surface. Finding her own self lost, she too became lost in the memories of the two of them together. The places they would go. The fun they shared. Leaning the rake she was using to weed the front flower beds against the fence, she went inside to sort through her bag. After several moments of not finding what she was looking for, it suddenly occurred to her where the item was. Collapsing down into an arm chair, she began sobbing and saying aloud to herself. "It was the only picture I had of you Samuel."

It was a difficult night. Where one was over joyed at the anticipation of seeing someone they could really see themselves with, the other plummeted into deep despair. Mary knew what she had to do when the sun came up, filtering it's rays through the still dirty windows of the tiny cottage.

"Claire? I have to leave." announced Mary.

Claire, smoothing out the blanket she used on the small bed that Ms. Edith brought to them both, looked up in surprise. "What? Why? We just arrived."

"Claire. I see how you feel about Alexander. And I know your feelings. Your thoughts. They are the same as I have for Samuel. Still have. I have to return back to America and look there. He's not here. I would have found him by now." Mary stated.

Claire nodded with understanding, taking her hand. "I understand Mary. I do. But you…you have to accept that, perhaps, perhaps Samuel is…" Claire trailed off here, not able to finish that despairing thought. Even though she had never met Samuel, just knowing Mary was enough to understand who he was. The thought of his death was saddening even to her. Regaining her composure, Claire continued. "But please, also understand I can not go. I really like him and we only spoke for less than five minutes."

"Say no more. I know. I know. You have to stay. And I hear you. I do. About Samuel I mean. And it's a real possibility. I may never, ever really know what happened to him. But right now. I'm being pulled to return home. I have to go." said Mary. Mary paused for a moment, looked away, saying, "I have to."

48

Finding Home

"How far up can I go on ten dollars for my wife and I?" asked Samuel as he slipped the money from a zippered pouch.

"Up to North Conway. That's in New Hampshire. There are only two other stops from there. Lincoln and Littleton. Littleton being an additional three dollars." replied the railroad clerk behind the window.

"I see. This...this North Conway place...it has hotels?" inquired Samuel.

"It does. They get the busiest during the winter season. Skiing and all. You looking for work? the clerk asked studying Samuel and Monique.

"I am. Yes." replied Samuel.

"Well then. I suggest the Mount Washington Hotel then. She's the grandest of them all in all of New England."

Samuel considered this then asked. "Do they have housing for their staff?"

"They do. On property. What with the golf course, stables, and all the events that are going on, they are always in search of good workers."

"If we went to this North Conway how would we get to this hotel?" asked Samuel.

"Easy enough. There are motorcars that will take guests all the way up to Bretton Woods. That's where the Mount Washington is located. Or, there "

"Well then. Two tickets for North Conway then." said Samuel. Samuel started to turn when Monique tugged on his arm, saying low. "The doll. Don't forget the doll." Turning back to the clerk he asked. "Almost forgot. Does the train pass through a place called Quincy before heading north? There's someone I need to find."

"Quincy? Yeah, yeah. It does. There's a lay over there for an hour." said the clerk.

"Perfect." Reaching into the bag he carried over his shoulder he pulled out the doll that Carl had given him and the address attached. "Any idea where I could find this address?"

The clerk looked at it shaking his head. "I don't know my around there much. Don't go there that often. I'm sure you'll find someone though at the stop."

The clerk make out the forms for two tickets, handing them to Samuel. Taking the tickets, Monique stood with her arm around his own, as they both looked at each other taking a deep breath. As they walked away from the ticket booth, he couldn't help but think of a familiarity in the place they were going to. Turning to Monique, "I think…I think I know this place."

"I know. I could tell when you were talking to the train clerk. They are memories. I think you've found your home. Or at least close to it." she replied in return as they walked along the north end of Boston.

Samuel nodded. "Perhaps. But there's something…I'm not sure what."

As they stood in the long passenger line Samuel couldn't help but feel the significance of taking that step aboard the train to a destination where he felt he had already been.

The city of Lynn was not far. The train pulled into the station, Samuel not wasting any time. "Are you alright to wait here?" he asked Monique. "Go. Go. I'm tired anyhow. I'll take a little nap while we are stopped. It's so hard to sleep at all when the train is moving."

Samuel got up from his seat, walking down the aisle. As he came to one of the conductors he asked. "How long will be here?"

"Forty five minutes mister. If you are getting off, don't wander far." said the conductor.

Unfolding the note with the address on it he read it to him. "Any idea where I can find Sweetser Terrace?" The conductor glanced at the address himself nodding. "That's up in the Wyoma Square area. On Flax Pond. Pretty area. If you are going there, you best be a pretty good runner."

"Which direction?" asked Samuel.

"That way there." replied the conductor.

Samuel hadn't done much running over the last couple of years. He surprised himself after the first half mile that he was still pretty good without getting winded. The army and basic training did something for him he thought chuckling to himself as he held tight to the shoulder bag with the doll and address inside. Stopping only to ask for quick directions he made his way up Broadway Street, passing a couple of schools, a ladder factory, several firehouses, and a vast cemetery that looked as though it went on for miles and miles. How many of those grave markers had names of soldiers who he may have known he thought. After twenty minutes he found a sign that read Flax Pond and jsut a couple of streets away Sweetser Terrace. Fifty one was the house number, as he slowed a bit to look at the numbers on the sides of front porches and doorways. It wasn't long before he found the house. Taking a deep breath he stepped up on the front steps and knocked on the door. After one additional knock, a middle aged man came to the door.

"Excuse me Sir. Good afternoon. I've come all the way from Paris, France and I think I have something that may belong to your family. Or your daughter? It's from Carl. He gave me this address and asked me to deliver it. There's a letter with it also." explained Samuel as he pulled out the doll with the attached envelope.

The man looked at him, oddly at first, studying him, then glancing to the doll, back again to Samuel. "You came from where? Paris?" the man said.

"Yes Sir. I was stationed there. Was wounded, hospitalized for almost a year. I'm just now making my way back home. At least I think I am…" Samuel trailed off. "No matter. I think I know your son Carl?

Samuel held the doll as a mother does her child, with a gentle embrace.

The man's eyes widened at this. "Carl? My boy? He's….your telling me…he's in Paris, France?"

"Yes Sir. That's where I met him anyway. He's working at an immigration office there. He gave me the doll here. Said it was his sister's. And that he carried it with him during the war. He asked me to do him a favor and return it." Samuel further explained.

The man half turned, calling over his shoulder. "Mary? Mary dear. Come here for a moment."

Samuel immediately felt uncomfortable. A sudden feeling of being out of place hit him. Perhaps it was seeing the young woman coming down from the stairs. He wasn't sure.

"Yes Daddy?" she said as she stood next to him looking directly at Samuel.

"This lad here says this is your doll. Is it?" the father asked.

"My doll! Yes! I gave this to Carl the day he shipped off to basic. But how…?" Mary stated as she looked to Samuel.

"Miss? With no disrespect. Your father will explain. I really don't have much more time to spend. I wish I did. But be assured, your brother gave me your doll personally to return back to you. He's well and living in Paris. Now if you'll excuse me, I really need to run back to the depot. My train will be leaving in …" Samuel went on, looking past the two in the doorway, noticing a wall clock. "…in fifteen minutes. It took me almost twenty five to get here. I need to go."

"Now now lad. Relax. We will drive you down to the station. It's only a few minutes. Along the way, you can fill us in with more details about Carl." said the father.

Instantly appearing more relaxed and that feeling of being uncomfortable gone almost as quick as it came, Samuel could only say, "Thank you."

Along the way, the three of them exchanged names, and the gratitude they each had for Samuel's promise fulfilled. In the short trip, Samuel learned a lot. Especially about Mary, Carl's sister. It wasn't anything specific, but just her name touched something inside of him. He remembered the night outside the hospital, near Notre Dame, where he watched the young couple at the gazebo. The feeling was like that, when he first whispered to himself her name. As he exited the car, he again thanked the father for his kindness. Turning his attention to his daughter, he thanked her as well, saying her name aloud, "Mary. Thank you." She turned her eyes away in a small blush momentarily, as she returned a deep, adoring smile back to him.

The train ride was not long. A bit noisy and bumpy, but bearable. What made it endurable wasn't Samuel's constant thinking of this new place and the beginning of making an entirely new home with Monique in a place he already knew, but far more importantly the expressions on Monique's face as the train distanced itself from the city and urban areas to see the looming mountains on the horizon take shape. Having been born and raised in Paris all of her life, the highest elevation she had ever been was at Montmarte, a mere four hundred thirty feet above sea level, and where he took her often. Even living in the country side of France for the past two years, there were only meadows and rolling hills of no real significance. As they both gazed out the windows, with the vast expanse of forests and the granite mountains becoming larger and more bolder before their eyes, the gain in elevation caused them to hold hands a little tighter; forefinger curled around the pinky, in their special way.

Leaving Paris in the springtime, to make a still chilly voyage across the Atlantic was leaving behind all that they knew. Her father knew it yet still offered his sincerest blessing, knowing that he may never see his daughter again or his grandchild. And as the train made its lolling way around the curves of the track to places still yet unknown, passing farmlands and wet marshes, fields in bloom, the jagged edged cliffs of granite that jutted out from smooth, lined surfaces succumbed in towering pines; the horizon disappearing when mountain passes seemed to entrap the mechanical, diesel vehicle between their folds, darkening the inside, cutting off the light from the sky above; Monique's pregnant body nestled beside his, a reassuring comfort that together, soon to be the three, these mountains that they passed, would indeed protect and provide for them. A new home. Wherever it was. Awaited.

"Monique? I have to tell you something. The doll. That I gave back to that family. When I was holding the doll, something…something happened. I think it was the dress. Something familiar. The pattern. Or perhaps just …I don't know. The doll itself."

"Maybe you have a sister who had a doll like it. And you maybe you use to play with her. With her dolls." Monique said gently and reassuringly like she always does.

Samuel considered that. "Mmm, perhaps."

49

Coming Home

The deepest, darkest of skies illuminated the vast and wide porch that wrapped around the grand and majestic hotel known as the Mt. Washington. Like the mountain it was named after, standing on that porch and looking out over the breadth of its gardens; looming oak, maple, and elm trees dotting the sloping and rolling expanse of fine, cut lawn; a presidential range that rises over it all, leaving the on-looker to gasp, and gasp again. The poet may write lines that come close to describe such beauty as it all is, but to stand outside under the porch roof, where the white alabaster, Grecian columns hold true; in the autumn, colors a-flame reach those mountains like an artists palette splayed with a lifetime of work. And so they stood. Newly arrived from an ancient city of lights. Immigrant and native born with no connection or identity to the place they now stood and looked out upon. They sat on cushioned, wicker porch furniture, feeling like a Duke and Duchess of a once upon kingdom in child imagination. With his hand resting on Monique's, he recited lost words he had no reasoning to which they came

"Men hang out their signs indicative of their respective trades; shoe makers hang out a gigantic shoe; jewelers a monster watch, and the dentist hangs out a gold tooth; but up in the Mountains of New Hampshire, God Almighty has hung out a sign to show that there He makes men."

Turning to her, "We'll hang our own sign here. And it will say home."

A tear formed, slowly forming the wet trail down her cheek. "I'd like that."

Under the stars of the Mount Washington, a majesty they both had no prior vision of seeing, came to them the formation of family and the start of their lives, a-fresh and new.

"That another letter from Mary, Frank?", asked the post office clerk as handed over his mail. Glancing through the various mail that was handed to him he said, "Looks that way. She's the only person I know all the way over in Paris."

"Hard to believe she has been gone for almost three years now. And that poor boy. Samuel. Samuel Anderson. I can still see them together all over town. They were real smitten on one another." replied the clerk.

"Mary's a strong woman now. Not the little girl we all once knew. I suspect I'll barely know her myself she's grown so." Frank said, opening the envelope. Turning he half glanced over his shoulder to the clerk. "You have a nice day now Edward."

Frank walked out of the post office building, stopping at the front porch of the Northern Hotel, where he leaned against the porch railing reading Mary's letter. The early morning to which he was accustomed also brought other folks our early. Carriage horses began lining the frontage of the hotel, readying guests for an early morning departure.

"Morning Dr. Thompson. Looks like it might be a bit bitter today." came the voice of Jim Evans, livery stable manager and carriage driver for the hotel.

Interrupting his concentration Mary's father turned. "Hmmm? Ohh yes. Yes. Feels like it Jim. You best bundle up while up on the carriage seat now. The last time I saw you in the office you didn't exactly like being there."

"I don't like needles Sir. What more can I say." Jim replied.

"Pull that collar up then." Frank chuckled as he moved on, focusing again on his daughters script. Starting over, he read.

Dearest Father,

I'm in England now having left Paris three days ago by train. I'm staying at a lovely boarding house run by a very kind lady named Mrs. Edith O'Shea. She runs a tight ship and is every bit of her Irish heritage. She's been very helpful getting my boarding passes together for the steamliner. Which is named the Alaska by the way, and I'll be porting in Boston this time next week. I do hope this post reaches you in time. I was assured it would. Now Daddy, no surprises please. You know how I despise those things. Besides, I'll be stopping at the Mount Washington first to visit with Evelyn. You remember her? We went riding often. She works at the stables there. It has been too long since our last ride. I miss it. Let my school girls know I am coming home please. Doria and Dolores will be pleased to hear that. And their little sister Irene, who is not so little anymore. I'll be arriving on Monday on the afternoon train. I will see you soon Daddy. I miss you. And remember, no surprises.

Your Loving Daughter,
Mary

Finding himself half-way down main street, he folded up the letter, tucking it safely away into the inside pocket of his jacket. "You are coming home my dear." he said smirking to himself. "That's worth a celebration."

She rode in the motorcar up the graveled approach road to the grand hotel the same as she once did years before when young. This time she was no longer that little girl with curls and ribbons but a young woman who has traveled overseas, living and working with those who were in need of a tender hand, touch, and an unselfish heart that came natural; second nature. She realized, as she sat staring at the open spaces of well manicured lawns, hedges; fragrances of fresh cut, dew drenched grass, mingled with an October crispness in air, maples and oaks in full display of brilliance; red and orange fiery blazes, that her young heart was still in search of the one who first put light to her passions and desires. It was all just as she remembered. And it felt like home.

And it was like a passage into yesteryear of elegance, of class and grandeur, with women in petticoats, white gloves and gowns, men in top hats, tails, all dressed fancy for all occasions. She once had an innocent mind with a frame of hope and future. Merriment and excitement of celebrations with family, friends, and good company; a finger of scotch and champagne toasts. Giggles and whispers of gossip and making glee within the young women's circle. It was a whole lot of glamour mixed with a touch of mystery. And how she missed it so. As a young woman, riding equestrian events, weekends of feeling a sophistication, head held a bit higher than usual with a more delicate step, hoping to be seen by the handsome young men. The Mount Washington Hotel became her escape from small town living and going to school with bedraggled boys and silly girls who whispered behind your back. The solid white pillars aligning the grand wrap around porch was a memory revisited when she and her father first put feet on the porch boards, walking through the front door and into a luxurious world of fine architectural splendor. The grand staircase made her gasp and the grandfather clock chiming noon startling her in awe. A couple nights stay, then further north through the notch, and she would be truly home. The house atop the hill, overlooking the train depot and the tiny town, where she could stand on her own front porch, and see Samuel's light shining bright in his third floor bedroom. Biting her lip and nodding to herself she was aware of the irony of her search and that missing piece and where she now at this station of her life. Pulling up to the front of the hotel, the driver held the door for her as she took a deep breath, stepping out, and into her next chapter.

"Yes Sir. I'm a hard worker and willing to do most anything Sir." Samuel told the personnel manager of the Mount Washington.

"You fought over seas in the big one? Been living in Paris for awhile have you? Pretty city. Always wanted to go." the hotel manager said in return.

"I did. Wish I could tell you more, but …I'd rather just not talk about that. And yes. Paris. It's where I met my wife. I worked for her father for almost three years or so. He ran a little city market." Samuel stated.

"You can speak French then?" he asked.

"A little. I understand it better. Good enough to keep me out of trouble while there. My wife of course was born there." Samuel explained.

"Well. That's a big plus for you. We are in need of foreign language speakers here. We get a lot of Canadians that come down for the holidays. Their French might be a little different though. Alright. Come by Monday and I'll put you to work. You and your wife can stay in the employees wing. Nothing fancy mind you. Three rooms and a bath." the manager said.

"That's perfect. Thank you so much Sir." Samuel said excitedly.

Samuel found Monique near the road that leads to the stables. When he hurried to her she was admiring a collection of colored leaves she was gathering. "Monique. I got a job. We can stay. I start on Monday." Samuel turned toward the large wing of the hotel, with its many windows running in lines of twenty or more four stories high. "And we get an apartment right here."

"That's wonderful Samuel." Monique said happily. It's a great day. And these leaves, I've never seen colors like these."

"Autumn in New England. One of the prettiest places to behold my dear. You are in for a real treat." Samuel told her as he wrapped an arm around her waist.

They walked about the grounds, hand in hand, stopping to collect the fresh fallen leaves that scattered the ground in sheer abundance. The hotel was busy, with motorcars and buses continuously making their way up the road. Guests, not unlike themselves, of all ages, wandered and strolled the grounds. As Samuel and Monique approached the pond at the front, a small white arched bridge seeming to draw them in. "Beautiful" Monique said catching her breath. "It's like a painting and we are a part of it." Monique leaned over the rail, her reflection a near perfect mirror image, with Samuel to her left. Leaning to her, Samuel whispered to her ear, "water."

"What?" she asked.

"Water. It's the magic behind our love." Samuel said.

Monique tilted her head a bit, a soft smile displaying across her face.

"Water." Samuel said, using the word like a magical wand that sets things in motion. Drawing closer to her, his mouth found hers, in a kiss that embraced them both with mutual desire. With his hand holding hers, and both their hands lying on their yet unborn baby, their lips moved together as they were meant to be. Smooth, effortlessly, and with an intentional satisfaction of tenderness and devotion. When they parted Monique whispered to his ear the same he did moments before. "Water." And they kissed again.

Unpacking, she couldn't help but tell everything about her time in Paris to Evelyn, who sat on the edge of the bed with eagerness at all she was saying. As best friends do, despite the almost four years since they last spent time together, they felt as comfortable as the day they first met; as though no time has passed at all.

"The work was difficult, but the staff I worked with were excellent and fun to be around. And the soldiers themselves, and there were lots and lots, many…each of them were so grateful for all of our help." Mary rattled on with a high pitch excitement.

"Were they cute? Come on Mary. I know you. There was at least one who caught your eye. No disrespect to you and Samuel of course. But we are …women after all. And sometimes some boy comes along and makes us feel all warm." said Evelyn with a teasing tone.

Mary blushed. "Are you blushing?" asked Evelyn.

"I am not. Well, …not…alright already. Maybe I am. And maybe there was. But I'm not telling that part to you. I'll hear an entirely different version by tomorrow morning if I do." said Mary in return as she tossed a pillow at her friend.

"You know me so well." Evelyn replied back with a smug look and a laugh. "It's good to have you back again love. How long are you staying? Say for the week. Please. So we can ride everyday. I have a new horse you will just love. And Arabella is still here?" explained Evelyn.

"Arabella? She is still here? Well, I told Daddy I'd be arriving back to town on Monday afternoon, but I'm actually leaving Sunday afternoon. They're still running the late train on Sundays aren't they?" asked Mary.

"They are. But why so short? When will you be back?" asked Evelyn taken back a little with a genuine sadness in her voice.

"You know my father. He will insist on having a celebration, a surprise one at that. I told him Monday but I will arrive on Sunday to avoid all of that. He knows I so despise surprises. Especially with the entire town at my house. All I want is to go home where it is quiet and take a deep, long breath." Mary explained.

"That's understandable love. I have next weekend off. I'll make the trip up and we will spend it together. How will that be?" Evelyn asked.

"Perfect. And thanks for understanding. Does the church still have a Sunday service? I think I would really like to go before setting out." Mary inquired.

"They do. The congregation come here for brunch afterwards. Sunday mornings and early afternoon are always busy here." said Evelyn.

There was a silence between the two young women just then. A momentary pause between two friends who shared more interests then they knew and wished for the same things as young women then they cared to admit. It was Mary who broke the silence happily.

"Let's go riding!" and with that she stopped everything she was doing, grabbing her friends hand, running toward the door and down the hallway.

"That's the Mary I know. How I have missed you." shouted Evelyn with an equal amount of enthusiasm.

The back meadow was just as she remembered it. She and Evelyn rode for hours through the trails that ran along side the south to north train tracks. Passing the depot not so far away she stopped to make inquiry about the Sunday departure time. That hadn't changed either. The same time and train she and her dad would take back home after a weekend of riding.

"Well, things certainly haven't changed much." she said aloud giggling. "Typical New England."

A little further down they rode past Our Lady of the Mountains church. Checking the Sunday mass hours, that too hadn't changed. Eight thirty AM. But perhaps the most striking detail of the ride that made her feel like she was really home, was the mighty Ammonoosuc River that meandered its way to their right the entire time. The same river where she and Samuel first met and the very same where they spent so much time together in the middle of town. The sound of its waters rushing over scattered rocks with the occasional sightings of folks fishing. The longing to see her father made her heart ache a little more. This time tomorrow she would be standing in the middle of her living room as his reassuring and protective arms wrapped his only daughter. She realized she was making the right choice in returning.

"Evelyn, this has been delightful. And you'll be up in two weeks? We will have quite the time and more time to catch up, I promise." Mary told her best friend as the two walked their horses to the stalls.

"Of course. Tomorrow night, I will just have to dance with all the handsome boys by myself. There's a wonderful jazz band playing." Evelyn said in a tone meant to make Mary envious.

"I am sure you will. But I will be home."

"Then we will ride to church together then." said Evelyn.

The next morning, Mary made her way to the stables for the second time in twenty four hours. Evelyn had both horses ready. "Let's take these animals to church." she said with enthusiasm. "Race ya." replied Mary.

They awoke to a rain shower. It fell with soft pattering against the windows, streaming droplets making the view just a little distorted. Peering out Monique was captivated by the beauty of the mountains around them, even with low lying, gray clouds and mist. Looking closer, down the front lawn and near the river, a lone building of some sort stood through the rain. "Samuel? Samuel. I think that's a steeple." said Monique as she tried peering ever closer. "It is. It's a church Samuel. We should go."

"It's raining love." said Samuel still a little groggy from sleep.

"It's not raining hard. Just a shower. Come on get dressed. We can pretend its Notre Dame." she said.

They didn't have anything proper for rain. Samuel put on an overcoat that would surely soak through quickly and Moniquie a shawl from her grandmother with a coat that would surely be too warm for the time of year over that. Descending the stairs from the employees housing, they did find an umbrella on a makeshift coat rack. Looking to one another suspiciously and full of tom foolery, they both giggled as they lifted it off the hook, stepping out into the rain and splashing their way to the front road which they had not twenty four hours earlier made their way up the first time.

It was a light rain, not really heavy, and not really cold for the autumn season, but rather just right, left to make one soak in a golden yellow morning as the sun peeked in and out of the slow moving clouds. Holding hands, in their special way, passenger motorcars passed them by, either making their way to the front of the hotel or leaving, both cases true destinations unknown.

"Where do you suppose all these people are going off to? And where have they come from?" Monique asked as they walked.

"I suspect most are not too much unlike ourselves. Finding a new place, exploring, taking a chance in a new way of life." Samuel replied, then adding. "Perhaps returning to an old one."

There was a brief pause between the two, as there often is, neither having need to answer quickly or directly when in conversation, but giving the other the time to respond or not respond, a reciprocity grounded in a connection that is undeniable. "I'm glad we are together. Us. Doing all of this." Monique said, squeezing Samuel's hand a little tighter while placing a hand over their baby. Samuel lifted her hand placing a single, gentle kiss and just smiled.

Reaching the end of the approach road, they could see the steeple of the church just over the horizon. "Must be a couple of miles at least." said Samuel.

"Then it's just like when we lived in the village when we moved away from Paris together. We would walk two miles to the market once a week together. It will be like that. And I haven't been in a church for a long time." said Monique.

"Well. I don't ever remember being in one at all." said Samuel laughing aloud.

"We best fix that quickly then Sir." Monique replied.

They walked together. hand in hand, almost always hand in hand, until the church presented itself in front of them. The peaked gambrel roof that held the holy cross atop, was identical and larger than the smaller below it, with large windows that reflected the mountains even in the rain. The alcove to the left was the location of two fifteen foot arched doors leading into the quaint church setback in the towering pines. As Samuel and Monique approached, now thoroughly wet, they noticed a lone horse tethered to a railing at the front entrance. Picking up her pace, tugging Samuel along, Monique made her way to the horse, where she immediately made her fondness known. "Ohh, Samuel. She's beautiful. I use to ride. Did I tell you. Father and Mother and I. I was very young, and I would take turns sitting with them both. They'd let me hold the reins." Monique described with an excitement in her voice. "Riding is the best memory I have of mother." Letting go of his hand, she walked around the horse, petting her mane, brushing her between splayed fingers, running a finger down her nose. Noticing an engraving on the harness, she read, "Arabella. What a lovely name for such a fine animal." With her mind elsewhere, Samuel watched her, then slowly approached. Slowly, reaching out his hand, he too touched her. "Arabella" he said to himself, in barely a whisper. Then again, "Arabella." This time followed by "Mary" loud enough for Monique to hear.

"What's that?" she asked, interrupted from her remembrance.

"Arabella. That was her name." Samuel replied with a hesitant and rather shivering voice.

"Whose name?" Monique asked, moving to him, with a hint of concern.

"Her horse's name. It was…Mary's horse. She named her Arabella." said Samuel startled, with a sudden and impacting realization of what it all meant. "Monique? Darling. I think Mary may have been my wife? Or girlfriend? She's here."

Samuel became frantic in his stance then, moving and shifting from foot to foot, looking around about with rapidity and nervousness.

"Samuel? Are you sure. This horse…" Monique began, holding the horses harness, her hand over the engraved name.

Samuel nodded. "I'm sure." Leaving her side, he stepped quickly to the doors of the church, where he placed his hand on the handle. Monique followed, beside her husband. Opening the door, he peered in at the nearly vacant room. Only a handful of people sat, mostly at the front, with two at the end pews in the back. Monique came in after, closing the door behind her, as the noise of the rain outside echoed its smooth pattering inside, causing some to turn around. And there she was. Like a long lost friend rediscovered she just appeared. In a rush of tumult unexpected excitement, and like a flooding of his senses to every extreme, it all came back to him. Mary was there. In front of him. A woman now, a young girl of only eighteen then, who he left to leave for a place he knew nothing about fighting for people he never met. He realized he loved her. Or did. At one time. Perhaps still does. Monique stood beside him, as her hand reached for his, more to steady him then to claim him, for she knew too the implications of this very unexpected meeting. One that would surely change their lives. Placing a hand over their baby, she reached out to a handrail to steady herself as well.

50

Reuniting

Evelyn sat atop her own horse while holding Arabellas reins. With her other hand, she held her best friends hand. "Are you sure Mary? You're alright?" she asked with deep concern.

"I am Ev. I am." Mary replied, tilting her head upward then adding. "Actually, for the first time in a very, very long time I feel better than just alright."

Peering over to Samuel and Monique, seeing him as she remembered him, only a little older, she nodded. "Alright then. But I'll be up in a couple of days. I am not waiting until the weekend."

Mary smiled up to her letting go of her hand. Turning toward Samuel and his wife, Evelyn turned both horses back toward the majestic Mount Washington.

Standing before them both, she looked to Samuel first and then over to Monique. With a half step and leaning, she reached out her hand toward her. "Hello. My name is Mary."

The train station was just down the road not far from the church. The rain had let up so the walk was both done in silence broken with Samuel's recollections. "I use to go to church here. With my mother and father. I was only a little boy." And then, when they arrived at the train depot, "And father and I would ride the train together. Once a week. And stay...there." Looking over his shoulder, he could just make out the hotel from whence they came. Long stretch of pauses would ensue. "And we would return...to...Littleton...back home."

It came back to him in such flooding remembrances it felt both overwhelming, where Monique and Mary both had to place their arms around him to steady at him, to a sense of elation of finality where he would sit in the cushioned seat of the train, exhaling slowly and smiling and smiling.

Turning to Mary for the first time, "I'm going home aren't I?" She nodded to him as Monique held his hand. "Mmmm. You are."

The ride was not long. Only a couple of hours with three short stops at other depots along the northward bound rail. When they arrived at the Littleton depot, it was a little before the noon hour. The three of them stepped out of the passenger car with perhaps twenty others, standing on the dock together. "The river is near here." Samuel exclaimed. Quickly turning and striding away from the two women, he made his way in front of the engine and to the street. Looking down the street he turned back to the two, who were trying their best to keep up, while Mary held Monique's arm. "It's down there. The river. Isn't it? The river is just down there. And…and…" Samuel began. "And up there. On that hillside. That's….", peering closer in a squint through the autumn sunlight, "…that's where I live. My father's hotel!" Turning on hell, he looked past the Mary and Monique. "And up there…that's….that's your house Mary! I walked you home from school everyday." he said with a hearty laugh.

Mary and Monique turned to each other and laughed. What more could they do. Watching Samuel was like watching a six year old opening his gifts at Christmas.

"Where would you like to go first Samuel? To see your father? Walk around town? Or …perhaps to my house? Right up there." Mary asked him.

Samuel thought. This struck him hard. Meeting his father. "My father? I'm not sure. I think…I think I need some time on that. Monique? What do you think?" he asked his wife.

Monique turned to Mary. "I think I would like to go to the closest place. I am almost eight months before delivering our baby." she said with a chuckle. Mary laughed as well.

"That takes care of that then. Then pregnant woman wins." said Mary.

"There's a dirt path right over here." said Samuel as they walked along the South Street sidewalk. "I would take it to get to your house quicker."

Mary had so many questions going through her own head she wanted to ask him. But she knew, after having worked with so many other soldiers who experienced all kinds of medical problems, some that did include memory loss, short term as they were, that flooding him with questions could very well lead to a shutting down of the memories that were returning. Samuel was alive and back and that was all that was important right now.

"My father is not at home right now. So it will be quiet. He always goes to lunch with friends after church on Sundays. Besides, he thinks I am arriving on Monday so I could avoid a big celebration that he is famous for." Mary giggled.

Approaching her house, Samuel's attention was directly in front of him. Peering upward, he said, "That's your bedroom. Up there. I could see your light at night from my own."

"That's right. And I could see yours as well." Mary replied.

Monique was quiet. She had no words of what had just transpired. It all felt so unreal. They went from Paris to New Hampshire in less than two weeks and Samuel is remembering everything as though it was yesterday just by Mary's presence. She loved him. She was in love with him. And she was carrying their child. This was to be their home and she supposed still could be but was nervous and unsure of just how everything was not only going to transpire but how three of them, soon to be four, were to fit in with each of their lives. It was obvious Mary still had a hold over him.

Stepping on the front porch, Samuel turned then to take a look around. The town itself came into full view. The buildings along main street, the high school he attended, and to the right of that, high on the hill, the hotel which he called home. And then there was the river itself. The Mighty Ammonoosuc that flowed through the center of the nestled town that thrived between two hillsides. The river where he had first met Mary. He closed his eyes for a moment, taking it all in, blinding himself, shutting out all other sounds around him. That was the moment he realized he was home. He was brought back just then by the front door opening and a shout of voices saying, "Surprise Mary!" As he turned, he saw a dozen or more people at the entrance of the doorway, peering out, with glasses in hand in toast. They were all smiling to Mary as their attention turned to the two standing behind her. Her father stepped forward, hugging his daughter. And then he saw him. His own father. And they looked to each other. His father wept. He wept. And like a wave that crashes against the cliff sides along an oceans coast, all of his inner turmoil from the war he never knew he carried eroded away all at once. Walking to his father, he took his hands in his, motioning for Monique. Going to him, he said, "Father. This is Monique. And this is your grandchild." The other guests were stunned, realizing who the young man was. Then a raucous roar of celebration and tears erupted. Mary's father, Samuel's father, both son and daughter, and Monique and baby, wrapped their arms around each other. Looking to Mary, Samuel whispered to her. "Thank you." Whispering back to him, "Yes" Mary squeezed his shoulder then shouted, "Welcome to Samuel and Monique." The gatherers then erupted into "Welcome home Mary and Samuel and Monique." followed by "and little one". Laughter was all around him. Feeling a hand on his shoulder, he turned then, to see an old man standing before him. "Ishmae" said Samuel.

Noticeably older, with a full, gray beard, the lines in his face were more distinguishing of character than ones of old age.

"You have completed your first circle." Ishmae said in return, smiling to the man who he delivered into the world. And the two embraced.

51

Conclusion

Samuel and Monique and Mary climbed the grassy slope not out of necessity but in hope of finding the horizon at the top. A horizon that may lend some kind of semblance toward the direction and the destination which they were traveling. The climb itself was not strenuous nor of a technical difficulty, for both were experienced, not just with the endeavor, but with life's own climbs as well. Like a metaphor, the climbs of growing pains, relationships, and the overall circumstances of merely living. They sought a sign, a promise. A promise that the path they followed, haphazardly or one with intent, was one of conviction, surety, and a confidence that would instill all they wanted. So they climbed. And the summit was reached. And on that summit a lone tree stood. A sentinel of time that had weathered many a storm. Charred by lightning, singed by fire, scarred by pestilence. The lone apple tree was all that was left of Mary's orchard so long ago. The home of her mother and where she felt the closest to her.

As the three of them stood before it, the path behind them in the past, the path ahead the future, Samuel and Mary held hands, in their special way, a quiet homage to those cherished and a mournful yearning to those gone, while he and Monique the same with his other hand. And in that quiet, that moment, in a solitude of nature that was undeniable, all around them, they found the answer. For on the trunk of that tree a faint outline of an etched heart that read but one word: "yes". Overcome and overwhelmed with elation, Mary stepped forward, placing her hand at its center. Feeling the engraved roughness, wielded by his knife so many years ago, she swore she felt the tree gasp just then, letting out a soft sigh of first despair but then relief. And they became one She and the old one. Not just a tree but a living entity of a time before. She felt all of its joys, triumphs, and pains as well. Her mouth drew in awe as her lips whispered "yes". A word with no question attached or context in meaning. A word on its own left to interpretation and to stand the test of time. The energy of that moment grew, passing through her and into him. Her hand still curled in his. He knew her thoughts, her dreams, her desires and loves. Like a veiled fog that lifts with a warming air, he realized then their Fate was tethered to their Destiny with the tree as their anchor. Turning to Monique, they repeated what the tree taught them: 'Yes'. And like a poet who writes lines of adoration, a breeze crept up over the slope, caressing them both with a verse that would move them ahead with rhythm and rhyme.

And so it was. Samuel and Mary and now Monique, stood together, on a hillside that overlooked the tiny hometown where they first met, and found love within each other.

Samuel turned to each of his loves then, addressing them both with equal attention. "To be loved at your worst is, I think, what true love is."

...

Epilogue

Afterword

"Finding Water" is written in a series of scenes from the characters' lives. This is done on purpose and in deep regard for the reader. Coming of age stories, like "Finding Water" will often invoke powerful memories, such as hometowns and lost loves almost forgotten. As each person has their own individual story, filled with their own experiences and memories, "Finding Water" allows the insertion of those experiences into the story. In this way, the reader becomes more involved, stopping from time to time in recollection, and perhaps saying to themselves, "That was me." or "It was like that." When that happens, it is perhaps the most powerful moment for the reader, for they become fully immersed in the happenings of the characters lives, with the ability to relate and even relive a part of themselves. It is with the authors personal gift to give to others those times again.

"Finding Water" is the first in a series that will chronicle the historical timeline of the small town setting of Littleton, N.H. and the White Mountains of New Hampshire while paying attention to the news of the world and the histories that moved people socially and emotionally. With important details for family traditions and cultural understanding, "Finding Water" will, in hopes, leave the reader with a sense of place and human connection.

Made in the USA
Columbia, SC
10 January 2025

d207a5e7-59de-4cf6-b10e-1f9befac8bdcR01